THE
PAUPERS' CRYPT

MOVING IN SERIES BOOK 5

RON RIPLEY

EDITED BY EMMA SALAM AND LANCE PIAO

ISBN: 979-8-89476-015-5
Copyright © 2016 by ScareStreet.com

ENTER THE REALM OF TERROR...

We'd like to take a moment to thank you for your support and invite you to join our VIP newsletter.

Dive deeper into the darkness with exclusive offers, early access to new releases, and bone-chilling deals when you sign up at www.ScareStreet.com.

Let the nightmares begin...

See you in the shadows,
Scare Street

CHAPTER 1
WORKING AT A NEW JOB

Brian had worked at a few places in his life. Ghostbusting, as it were, had been interesting, fun, and dangerous as hell.

But Rye, New Hampshire, and the dead Japanese had been too much.

Brian decided he didn't want to have another heart attack. The next one, he was fairly certain, would put him in the ground. Jenny agreed.

Nearly three months had passed since the last brutal deaths and mutilations. Brian hadn't gone on any more jobs, and he hadn't heard from Leo either.

Which was fine with him.

But since dealing with the violent dead was too stressful, he decided he wasn't going to be a ghost hunter anymore. Which meant he wouldn't dip his hands into Leo's bank account anymore either. Brian needed to find a job that wouldn't stress him out, and preferably one where he didn't have to deal with many people.

He and Jenny had talked it over, and when the superintendent job at Woods Cemetery in Mont Vernon had popped up, Brian had applied. He had gotten the job as well. It was, for the most part, a one-man deal. Make sure the cemetery office was open Monday through Friday, seven to three. Saturday, eight to twelve. He also had to keep in touch with the town's maintenance crew so they could trim the grass, cut back trees, and do whatever other work was required. Brian would be no more than a glorified custodian.

It was perfect.

In fact, Jenny would drop him off on her way to work, and pick him up at four. He didn't mind the extra hour. Brian planned to write during that time. He had a couple of good ideas for horror stories.

"Ready, sleepyhead?" Jenny asked, walking into the parlor.

"Hm?" Brian asked, looking up and smiling at her.

"Ready for your first day at work, babe?" she asked. Her face was absolutely glowing; she was thrilled with his early retirement from ghost work.

"Yeah," Brian said with a grin as he stood up. "I'm ready."

He picked up his travel coffee mug off the side table, stuffed his copy of *'Salem's Lot* into his jacket pocket and followed Jenny out and onto the porch. He waited as she locked up, and then slapped her on the behind as they went down the stairs.

"Hey!" she said playfully. "You're frisky this morning."

"Just excited about the new job," Brian said, getting into the passenger seat of her car.

She raised an eyebrow as she started the car. After she had backed out and shifted into drive, she glanced at him and asked, "What's going to happen if there are ghosts wandering around the cemetery?"

"I'm going to ignore them," Brian said, putting his coffee down in the cup holder. "Absolutely, positively going to ignore the *hell* out of them. They do not need to know I can see or speak with them. I am looking forward to a job filled with peace, quiet, and only living people to occasionally speak with."

Jenny smiled at him. "Good."

She turned on her iPod, synced it with the car, and soon they had Social Distortion blasting through the speakers.

Brian grinned and relaxed into the seat. *Today is going to be a good day.*

They made it all the way through the song *Bad Luck* before Jenny turned on to Partridge Road and came to a stop at the gate to Woods Cemetery.

"Ready for your first day of school?" she asked teasingly.

"You know it," Brian replied.

Jenny shook her head and laughed.

He leaned over, gave her a kiss and said, "I'll see you at four, babe."

"Yes, you will," she said, grinning. "I love you."

"Love you, too," he said.

Brian grabbed his coffee, got out of the car and closed the door before he waved goodbye. He watched her until she turned onto Elwood Drive, and he went over to the gate. It was made of wrought iron, as was the entire fence, and it had a large, heavy chain and lock on it.

Brian fished out the key ring he had been given the day before when he'd stopped at the town hall, and found the right one for the lock. He put his mug on the ground and opened the gate. Brian looped the chain and lock through one of the gates, retrieved his coffee and looked out at the graves.

Woods Cemetery was small and beautiful. Tall oaks and elms lined the thin, ribbon of asphalt proudly labeled a road. To the right of the gate, with its own small driveway, was a one room shack with the glorious title of "Woods Cemetery Office."

My kingdom, Brian thought with a grin.

An old farmer's mailbox painted bright white stood to the left of the door. The mailbox was large enough to hide a small child in. The idea broadened the already large grin on his face, and he chuckled as he unlocked the door and let himself into his office.

He stood there for a moment, took a sip of his coffee, and looked at the room in front of him. Tall, thin filing cabinets lined the left and right walls while a small, roll-top desk was placed directly beneath the window. The back wall contained a pair of doors, one conveniently marked 'Bathroom' and the other 'Closet,' as well as a map of the cemetery. Brian suspected it was older than he was.

Brian realized there was no computer on the desk. Just a notepad, some pencils and a sharpener, a green-shaded desk lamp, and a rotary phone. An honest to goodness *black* rotary phone. There was, however, a rather comfortable looking chair, and Brian walked to it, pulled it out, and sat down.

And yes, ladies and gentlemen, he thought, *it is as comfortable as it looks.*

Brian looked around the office, smiled to himself and looked through the desk. He found a folder which listed important phone numbers for the town and state. There was also a telephone book from 2010. When he opened the center drawer, metal clattered against metal, which turned out to be a second key ring. This ring had two keys. Each was marked with masking tape. In neat letters, one was labeled as 'Crypt, Outer,' the second 'Crypt, Inner.' Brian held the keys in his hand and looked at them.

Finally, he stood up, went across the short room to the back wall and looked at the map tacked between the closet and the bathroom. It showed the cemetery was divided into seven sections, each numbered accordingly. At the far right corner, though, which corresponded to the hill at the back of the cemetery, there was 'The Paupers' Crypt.'

Brian looked at the keys in his hand and wondered, *When was the last time anyone was laid to rest in there?*

He added the key ring to the one given to him by Barbara Coryelle, the town manager, and went back to the desk. After he had picked up his mug, he lifted the receiver on the phone and was surprised to hear a dial-tone.

Guess it's not a decoration, after all, he thought, chuckling to himself. He returned the phone to its cradle, opened the door and stepped out into the spring air.

It was colder than when he and Jenny had left the house, and clouds had begun to gather along the northern part of the skyline.

Don't remember any rain for today, Brian thought.

With a shrug, he closed the door and decided to walk the perimeter of the cemetery.

Today, Brian decided, smiling happily, *today is going to be a good day.*

CHAPTER 2
JOHN LEE GOES FOR A VISIT,
7:30 AM, MAY 2ND, 2016

Thirteen days had passed since Emily had died.

John still couldn't sleep without half a bottle of vodka in him. It would kill him eventually, and as much as Emily would have hated it, John didn't mind the idea of it.

He had shaved for the first time since the funeral, and his face felt raw in the cool, May breeze. The jacket he wore was the thick, fleece-lined flannel she had bought for him, ten years before. Here and there the coat had been repaired, the small, neat stitches a constant reminder of Emily's careful, beautiful personality.

John fished a pack of American Spirit cigarettes out of his breast pocket, lit up and stared at the cemetery.

She'd be so angry if she could see me smoking, John thought. He exhaled a long, steady stream into the morning air.

She had helped rid him of all of his vices. Not in a nagging way. Never nagging. Care and love. Things John never had much of before Emily.

But the cigarettes and the alcohol helped him deal with her loss. They were crutches, he knew, but they were familiar ones. Old friends half-forgotten with age. John was seventy years old, and his continued existence was a testament to Emily's love, and to the blind eye of a malignant God.

Sinners in the hands of an angry God, John thought, remembering his Jonathan Edwards. He fought the urge to blame God for Emily's death. To blame anyone or anything for her death.

But her heart had given out. Nothing more, and certainly nothing less.

John sighed and smoked while standing outside the entrance to Woods Cemetery. Emily's headstone had been delivered the day before, and the company, which was out of Nashua, had called and left a message at seven in the morning. John would be damned if he wasn't shaved before he visited her. Didn't matter if she was dead or not; Emily had never seen him up and out of bed without a shave.

And he wouldn't stand at her graveside with a cigarette in his mouth either. He threw it down, crushed it out on the old, cracked asphalt. Self-consciously he brushed at his jacket, swept his fingers through his still damp, silver hair, and then he stuffed his hands into his pockets before he stepped over the invisible threshold and into the cemetery.

As he did so, it felt as though the temperature plummeted ten degrees. He shivered, pulled his head further into the collar, and glanced at the cemetery office off to the right. There was a light on in the sole window, and a man was bent over, probably at a desk.

Good to know someone's here at least, John thought.

He turned his attention back to the cemetery. As he started to walk along the battered old road, he felt uncomfortable, as though someone sat in darkness and watched him.

John's skin crawled, and he looked around several times. Yet he couldn't see or hear anyone else. Beyond the iron fence, however, a late morning ground fog had sprouted up. The marshes beyond the perimeter were undoubtedly the culprit, but nevertheless, it was an eerie and uncomfortable sight. It almost looked like someone had a special effects machine which had been turned on and left to run.

John shook his head and focused his thoughts on Emily, on her grave. Within a few minutes, he reached her burial spot. The marker was there.

Emily Ann Lee
Beloved Wife of John, Salve for his Soul
Born June 6, 1946
Died April 20, 2016

The stone was a pale pink, her favorite color.

He tried to think of something to say. Anything. John knew it didn't matter. She was dead. She couldn't hear him. And what could he say?

A flicker of motion caught his eye and he turned away from the ground which covered his beloved wife to the stone, so recently, placed there.

Nothing, he scolded himself. *You're getting old.*

But as he turned away, something moved again. John looked back and caught a glimpse of white within the headstone itself.

A trick of the light, John said, yet even as the thought came, he realized there was no visible sun. The northern clouds had swept in and hidden the great day star.

Suddenly, there was motion and a quick flash of white. John straightened up, stepped back and tried not to call out in surprise and shock.

The white he had seen was a hand. A hand pressed against the flat surface of the stone, from the inside. As quickly as he had seen it, though, it had disappeared.

You're going crazy, he told himself. *Too much vodka. You're pickling yourself.*

Before he could retort, the hand appeared again. And he recognized it.

It was Emily's hand.

Pale and terrible to look upon, the palm continued to press upon the stone as though it were a piece of glass. John stared in shock, unable to look away.

Then, her second hand appeared. The marker groaned as she pushed against it, the polished granite bowing outward slightly. Faintly, horribly, she mouthed his name. Emily's face suddenly pressed against the surface, the nose and lips flattened. Black, hollow eyes found his and a wicked, terrible smile spread across her once sweet face.

John staggered back, heard a high pitched scream and dully realized the noise was his own.

Chapter 3
Brian's First Challenge,
7:35 AM, May 2nd, 2016

Brian was nearly halfway through his coffee when he realized there was no coffee machine in the office. There wasn't even a microwave. He hadn't brought any food either, of course.

The Cozy Corner Convenience Store was just up the road, and he knew they sold coffee and food, he just didn't have any desire to walk.

Well, dummy, he told himself, *if you want either of them you're going to have to.*

Brian was about to tell himself to shut up when a horrified shriek interrupted his thoughts and the tranquility of his first day. His heart gave a mutinous beat, but quickly settled back into an appropriate rhythm. He stood up, made sure his cellphone was in his pocket and made his way out of the cemetery. Off to the far left, where the newer graves were, he saw a man stumble and fall.

Christ, Brian thought. He broke into a brisk walk since he couldn't safely muster much more, and he kept his eye on the man who had fallen. He took his cellphone out, ready to call for an ambulance if it was a medical emergency.

Brian kept his thoughts focused on the man, though, who scrambled backward.

"Hey!" Brian called out as he got nearer. "Are you alright?"

The man didn't answer. He didn't have to.

Brian saw what was wrong.

The fingers were long and spread wide, the nails a dark, brutal red. The stone itself pushed out from its center, a woman's pressed face there. The surface of the marker stretched out as if it was nothing more than cellophane.

Black eyes flickered over to Brian and sent a cold, hard shiver up his spine and down into his groin. She snarled at him, and the man on the ground managed to get to his feet.

Brian kept his eyes on the creature in the headstone, grabbed hold of the man's arm, and pulled him away.

"Come on," Brian said in a harsh whisper. "Let's go!"

The man didn't resist. Together, they backed away from the headstone.

The hands reached down to the earth, hooked into the sod and dug in. Horrified, Brian saw the muscles leap into definition on the thin arms.

Oh, Sweet Jesus, he thought. *She's trying to pull herself out.*

The woman's face continued to push through and for a heartbeat, it seemed as if she would succeed. Then, with a howl that echoed off of the trees and shook Brian to his bones, the woman snapped back into the stone, vanishing from sight.

Brian fought the urge to vomit, and instead, he reluctantly turned his back on the headstone and brought the man back to the office.

CHAPTER 4

IN THE OFFICE, 7:45 AM, MAY 2ND, 2016

John let the man guide him into a chair, and he sat there as the man took a side chair from the far wall and sat down across from him.

"How are you feeling?" the man asked.

John looked at him for a moment, his thoughts still jumbled from what he had just seen.

The man before him was fortyish, bald, and lean. He looked like he was a hard one, and John could appreciate that. He had known more than a few tough men in his time and had even been counted among them when he was younger. Wilder.

Before Emily.

John shook his head. "Not feeling well at all."

"Can't imagine you would be. Name's Brian. Brian Roy."

John shook it. "John Lee."

"Pleasure, although this is kind of a strange situation," Brian said.

John chuckled in spite of the dread which lingered in him. "A powerful understatement."

"So," Brian said, "do you have any idea what that was?"

"No. I know it looked like Emily, my wife." John looked at Brian and then he said, "But, you saw it, too?"

Brian nodded. "I did. I surely did."

John relaxed slightly, but the fear he felt increased. He swallowed nervously and asked, "Why? Why was she coming out? I mean, she couldn't have been buried alive, could she?"

"No," Brian said. "I'll find out, though. Today's my first day on the job, and. it looks like figuring out what the hell is going on is the first task."

"This is a hell of a way to start a new job," John said sympathetically.

"Yeah," Brian said. He stood up, looked out the window and frowned.

"Tell me I'm not crazy, but there was no fog this morning, right?"

"You're not crazy," John said. "The air did get colder, and pretty quick, too. Still doesn't explain why or how the fog could roll in that fast. Or be so thick."

Brian nodded, played with an iron ring on his right hand and locked the door to the office. He looked out the window again, shook his head and then he returned to his chair. The old frame creaked under Brian's weight, and he looked at John.

"Was this the first time you experienced something like this?" Brian asked.

"You mean my dead wife reaching out of her headstone to grab at me?" John asked.

Brian nodded.

"Yes," John said. "I can't remember even hearing of anything like this."

"Well," Brian said, sighing, "I've seen some strange things, but nothing, and I mean nothing, like that."

"You've got me there, friend," John said. "This is an all-around first for me in every sense of the word. I just stopped by to speak with her. Rather, speak to her."

"Understood," Brian said.

The phone on the desk rang.

A sharp, hard sound which filled the small office and stabbed at John's ears. He blinked and turned his head away.

Brian stood up, crossed the small room and answered the phone.

"Woods Cemetery, Brian Roy speaking," he said.

Someone responded, and Brian's face went deathly pale.

CHAPTER 5

THE CALL, 7:50 AM, MAY 2ND, 2016

Brian stood still and hoped he wouldn't faint. His blood pressure had dropped, and his lungs seemed empty of oxygen. And even as he was able to realize and comprehend all of it, the voice continued to speak. The terrible, hideous voice of nightmares.

"Hello, Mr. Roy." The voice was cold and hard, it grated on the nerves and reminded Brian of every bad dream and horrific experience he had ever suffered. It was worse than nails on a chalkboard, worse than the screams of a dying man.

Brian's hands shook.

"I can almost smell your fear through the phone lines," the voice whispered. Brian couldn't tell if the speaker was male or female. "You're terrified. And you should be. You're not supposed to be here.

"Woods Cemetery doesn't need a caretaker, or anyone else," the voice continued.

"We'll leave then," Brian managed to whisper hoarsely.

"Oh no," the voice said, chuckling. "It's far too late for leaving. You should never have come. Be careful out there, Mr. Roy, the fog is getting thicker." And the call ended.

Brian's mouth was dry as he hung up the phone. He looked out the window and saw the speaker had told him the truth.

Anything beyond the iron fence was hidden by the fog. His world had been shrunk to the size of the cemetery. The fog formed a barrier which followed the lines and angles of the cemetery's border with a sinister intelligence.

"John," Brian said, and he looked over at the older man.

For the first time, Brian noticed the huge scar on the right side of John's face. A mass of twisted and cratered flesh which consumed the entire cheek and part of the forehead. The man's short silver hair was swept back, and the right eye was a dark, red globe.

John smiled sardonically and nodded his head. "Just saw it?"

"I did," Brian confessed. "I've seen a hell of a lot worse, though. Did time as a forward observer. Saw a little combat."

John nodded and stood up. "Bad call?" he asked.

Brian nodded. "Really bad. Let's get out of here."

"Lead the way," John said, gesturing to the door. "Lead the way."

With a sigh, Brian stepped over to the door, unlocked it, and stepped out into the cold air. His breath rushed out in a great white cloud.

"Damn, it got cold," John muttered.

"It'll get colder," Brian said, shutting the door. He turned to walk to the gate and stopped.

In horror, he watched as the gates slammed closed.

"What the…" John asked, confused. "How in the hell did they close themselves?"

Before Brian could offer up any sort of an answer, the rattle of the chain interrupted him. The heavy steel links which he had so carefully looped around the cross piece of the left gate, only an hour earlier, moved of its own accord.

He watched, stunned as it moved with all of the grace and ease of a serpent, slid around and through the bars before it finally found its own end. For a brief moment, the lock dangled, open and free, and then it snapped through the end link and closed upon itself. The 'click' of the tumblers was nearly smothered by the fog.

"Oh Christ, we'll have to climb the fence," John said.

Brian put his hand on the man's arm, and when John looked at him, he shook his head.

"Why?" John asked.

"I don't think it would be the best thing," Brian answered, looking around. Shadows flickered in the headstones, shapes and figures. Darkness and flashes of white.

"Maybe not," John said, "But I can't stay here. Old as I am, I'll try my luck," John said, a note of stubbornness in his voice.

Brian dropped his hand and took a step back toward the safety of the office.

John looked around and then he walked forward. He passed close to an old and weathered headstone. The marker was slate, the inscription on it faded from centuries.

A hand, gray and foul to the eyes, shot out. The fingers were crooked, powerful and quick like a spider's as they snatched at John's leg.

Even as the dead thing latched onto the man, John let out a high pitched scream, one full of pain and terror.

Brian stepped forward, wary of his heart, and winced as John was pulled down. A second hand slipped out, met its mate and locked around the ankle. Again, John screamed, jerked his leg back and tried to free himself.

By the time Brian reached him, the hands had dragged John a few inches closer. Brian bent down, raised his right arm and smashed it into the dead thing's twisted fingers.

The iron ring met the ghost, and a blast of cold, putrid air knocked Brian backward. He stumbled, caught himself and dropped to a knee as John scrambled away.

Brian's head pounded with the ferocity of his heartbeat and John helped him to straighten up. Together, they made it back to the office, and slammed the door closed. Brian staggered to the side chair and plopped down on it, while John collapsed on the floor. While Brian fought to get his heart back under control, he watched as John pulled up his pant leg. A large swatch of flesh was bluish white, and John looked up in shock at Brian.

"What the hell is it?"

Brian leaned back while breathing slowly and answered, "It's frostbite, John."

CHAPTER 6

WHAT TO DO, 8:00 AM, MAY 2ND, 2016

Brian didn't want any more coffee.

He wanted whiskey. A lot of it.

He also didn't want to be at Woods Cemetery, but it seemed like he wasn't allowed a say about it.

"Anything out there?" John asked.

Brian turned away from the window. "Just the fog. Can't even see the sky. Just fence, trees, and headstones."

"Anything else?" John said hopefully.

Brian looked back out there, saw the strange shapes and images in the headstones, and shook his head. "Not unless you count whatever's in the markers."

"I don't," John said.

"Well," Brian said with a sigh. "We've got nothing, then."

He took his cellphone out, looked at it and saw he had no service. Angrily, he shoved it back into his pocket before he sat down again.

"How long have you lived in Mason, John?" he asked.

John dropped his pant leg and thought for a moment. "Thirty years, this coming August. My wife, Emily, she was from Mason. She had a secretary's position at Nashua Plastic, and I was a tool and die maker for the factory. We bought a house next to her parents since both of her folks were sick at the time. What about you?"

"Just about a year," Brian answered. "Manchester before Mason. I'm from New Hampshire, though. Anyway, it's neither here nor there. What I'm wondering, John, is have you heard anything about Woods Cemetery?"

"Before this morning," John said, "I would have asked what was there to hear. But I know what you mean, and no, there was never anything like this. I mean sure, all cemeteries and boneyards have their ghost stories; it's

New England. But, nothing like this."

Brian nodded his agreement.

"There were stories about the cemetery, nothing I gave any credence to," John continued. "Stories about the random person who was last seen taking a stroll through the place and never came out. People who came out and said they'd been trapped there for a year. But you never met the person, you understand?"

"Always the friend of a friend?" Brian asked.

John nodded. "Or it was someone's cousin or neighbor. Never an eye-witness."

"How many of these stories did you hear?" Brian said.

"About three," John said, thinking for a moment. "Maybe four. But we're talking over thirty years."

"I understand," Brian said.

John looked at him for a moment, and then he asked, "Did you know that thing, whatever it was, would let go when you punched it?"

"I did," Brian said.

"How?"

Brian held up his right hand and wiggled the finger with the iron ring. John frowned.

"This is iron," Brian said. "Stops the dead. Well, ghosts at least. I hope like hell it works on whatever these creatures are, too."

"What's special about iron?" John said.

"Good question," Brian responded. "There's a theory, and from what I've seen, it makes sense. See, ghosts use electromagnetic energy in order to manifest. Iron, since it's so pure and raw, is an excellent conductor. Basically, if a ghost comes into contact with iron, the energy is syphoned right out of them. Sort of like a lightning rod.

"Some other people in the field," Brian continued, "they figure it's why so many old cemeteries are fenced in with wrought iron."

"Have you used it, before?" John asked. "To stop ghosts?"

"Yes," Brian said after a moment. "More than once."

"What is it exactly you do for work?" John said.

"Did is a better question," Brian said. "I used to help people with ghost problems. But only for a little while. My heart literally cannot take the stress."

"Bum ticker?" John asked.

"Yup," Brian answered. He paused and scratched his head, "I just thought of something."

"What's that?"

"The iron fence around the cemetery," Brian said. "I wonder if it was done on purpose, to keep the dead in."

"If your theory is correct," John said, "then it would make sense."

"Our forefathers *were* a hell of a lot more practical when it came to this stuff than we were," Brian said.

Silence fell over them, and Brian wondered how they could get out of the cemetery. The question was, would any of the dead be able to leave their graves? They had already seen two ghosts or spirits or whatever they were. The damned things even reached out of their headstones.

If people have gotten out before, Brian wondered, *how did they do it?*

"John," Brian said.

John looked at him.

"Feel like keeping busy?" Brian asked.

"How so?" John asked.

"Well," Brian said, "I'm thinking if maybe people disappearing in the cemetery isn't a new thing, maybe there's a record of some kind."

John stood up. "It's not a big place."

"So there shouldn't be too many spots to hide it," Brian said.

"I like the sound of that," John said. "Where do you want to start?"

"I'll take the files on the left if you want the ones on the right," Brian replied.

"Fair enough," John agreed.

The two men went to their respective walls, and they started to look.

Brian focused on the top drawer of the far left cabinet, which was labeled "Section 1 – A thru D." Within the metal, he found row upon row of dark green hanging folders, each one with the legend "S.1" and then the person's name. Thus, the first file read, "S.1 Aaronson, Aaron A." In the file, was a small note card which listed the row number, along with the plot number, and who was buried on either side of Mr. Aaronson. It also included who had purchased the plot and the headstone.

Yet there was nothing else other than that. No information on what to do if the cemetery decided it was time to lock the new caretaker in.

Brian sighed, shook his head, and moved on to the next file.

And the next, and the next.

"Hey," John said, breaking the silence after nearly forty-five minutes.

"What's up?" Brian asked, turning around.

John held up a thin sheaf of papers kept together with a large paperclip. With a grin, he read, "*What to do when trapped in Woods Cemetery.*"

"Where did you find that?" Brian asked, closing the drawer he had been looking in.

"Section seven. Defoe, Daniel," John said.

"Someone sure had a sense of humor," Brian said.

"Yup," John agreed. He held the papers out to Brian. "You seem to know a lot more than I do about this stuff."

Brian took them with a nod. He went and sat down in the side chair while John limped back to the desk. Quietly, he flipped back the title page and read the first page aloud,

> "*If the fog has risen from the marshes, and the gates have closed and locked themselves, you must beware of the stones. The dead buried here are less than peaceful. They do not slumber in the embrace of our Heavenly Father. They remain bound to their flesh and are maddened by it.*
>
> "*Do not think of the office as a sanctuary. It will not keep out the dead for long. While the sill and threshold have been salted, and the nails which bind the building together are of iron, the dead always find their way in.*
>
> "*It is best for you to make your way to the Paupers' Crypt. This, however, is risky, for within the Crypt, the dead are awake. There are several places to hide amongst the Paupers, yet they will ferret you out should you remain there long. Find a place of safety in the Crypt. You may have to move*

from one place to another, try not to lose hope.

"Beware of the Man though, for He is a deceiver, and one who will seek your end with all of His abilities."

Brian looked up at John and saw the man's face was grim, his mouth set in a hard line. The scar had gone a deathly pale and Brian saw the murder and hate in the man's eyes.

"My Emily is trapped here," John said softly.

Brian could only nod his agreement.

"Read on," John said tightly.

Brian flipped the page and saw a drawing.

"It's a map," Brian said, showing it to John.

"Looks like a path through the graves to the crypt. And there's something written at the bottom. It says, '*Follow the path and stay in its center. The dead will reach for you, but along this way, you are safe.*' "

Brian turned to the last page.

"In the desk, you will find two keys. One for the outer door of the Crypt, and one for the inner door you shall come upon. Leave each unlocked as you pass, lest you become trapped, if you must flee."

"This," John said, "sounds absolutely terrible."

Brian turned back to the map, looked at John and said, "I couldn't agree more."

CHAPTER 7
RUNNING FOR IT, 8:50 AM, MAY 2ND, 2016

"Are you ready?" Brian asked him.

John looked at the younger man and laughed. "Hell no. Feels like something's biting my leg and trying to work it right out of the socket."

"You'll make it?" Brian said.

John gave him a hard grin. "Yes, I'll make it. Don't worry about it. At least now I know what to expect. Let's do it."

"Okay," Brian said. He took hold of the doorknob and swung the door wide open.

A flesh-biting cold came sweeping into the office. It set John's teeth on edge, and he shivered.

"Damn," Brian said in a low voice. "This is bad."

"True," John said.

Brian led the way out with the map in his hand. He glanced at John and said, "Alright, John, follow me."

John kept close to the man, who took a few steps, referred to the map, and then proceeded a little more.

On either side of them, John observed the headstones. They were spread out a little further than the others, and luckily so. On the other side of the cemetery's wrought iron fence, the fog moved, curling in upon itself as it traveled along the length of the metal barrier. Yet the fog never crossed to mingle among the markers.

From each stone, the dead peered. Men and women. Children, too. Various ages and different shaped faces. Yet, all of them bore expressions of malice and hate. Their dead black eyes remained fixed upon the men and John felt uncomfortable. The slightest misstep, just an inch or two to the right, John realized, and the dead would grab him. His leg ached steadily, and the thought of another cold-burn like it pumped fear into his stomach.

And what would happen if Brian couldn't get to you in time? John asked himself. *What if the next one was quicker, stronger than the first? What's waiting for you in those stones?*

For a moment, he wondered what it would be like to join Emily in her cell in the cemetery. He remembered her gentle touch, the smell of her hair, the way she would smile.

And then he saw the hatred in her face. The black eyes which had once been green.

His stomach threatened to revolt and cast up the oatmeal he had eaten for breakfast. With a dry mouth and a mutinous gut, John continued to follow Brian's slow and steady lead.

Time passed slowly, and while it felt as if an hour or two had fled by, his watch revealed it was only nine when they reached the crypt. John had never seen it. Never bothered to. Neither he nor Emily had been one to enjoy a stroll through a cemetery. Occasionally, they would visit her parents' graves, place flowers there and trim back some errant grass. But, it was a place of burial and sadness.

Especially when he had said goodbye to Emily.

A hand lashed out at John's foot, and he pulled it away quickly. He nearly tumbled but managed to keep his balance.

Brian stopped and looked back, concern on his face. "You okay?"

John nodded and caught his breath.

"Constance Woolson, here," he said, gesturing towards the headstone whose owner had tried to snatch him. "Seems like she wanted me to visit."

"Told her no?" Brian asked.

"Yup," John said.

"Good, let's get away from them and into the crypt," Brian said. He rolled the papers, stuffed them into a back pocket and fished out his keys. "Ready?"

"Let's go," John said.

Together they passed through the last of the headstone gauntlet and walked up to the crypt's door. It was a massive, iron affair with a couple of hinges as long as John's forearms. Brian pushed aside a small keyhole plate, slid the key in and turned it until the lock's tumblers fell into place.

The hinges groaned, and the door swung outward easily.

Once it was opened completely, the two men stood and looked into the darkness beyond.

"Don't suppose it has lights, does it?" John asked after a moment.

"Probably not," Brian said.

"Hell," John said, "this just keeps getting better and better."

"Evidently. Think we should wait until we absolutely have to go in there?" Brian asked. "I mean, the dead aren't exactly leaving their graves just yet. We may have a little bit of time."

Before John could agree with Brian, a noise interrupted him.

A laugh. A high, shrill laugh.

Both of them turned around and looked behind them, off towards the center of the cemetery. At first, John couldn't see anything other than the trees and the grass, the headstones and the thin road.

Then, without a word, Brian pointed.

John followed the line of sight and felt his heart skip more than a fair share of beats.

The laughter hadn't come from one person, or even two people. But four children, ones of various ages, had stepped out onto the road. Three were boys, and one was a girl. They were all dressed in what must have been their Sunday finest, although those Sundays had probably occurred shortly after the end of the Civil War. Their skin, John saw, was as gray as the hand which had grabbed him near the gate.

And their eyes just as black.

A foul, nose-burning stench came racing along the cold air to him, and John took an involuntary step backward.

One of the boys laughed, and the children began to run towards them.

Brian grabbed hold of his arm and yelled, "Inside! *Now!*"

John nodded his agreement.

CHAPTER 8

INSIDE THE CRYPT, 9:03 AM, MAY 2ND, 2016

Brian let go of John, turned around, took hold of a small handle and pulled on the door. Normally, he would have wondered about a handle on the interior of a crypt, but now he was thankful for its existence.

The dead children, their hair a polluted brown and free in the air, shouted and laughed as they gained ground.

Brian finally managed to get the door closed, and the happy laughter of the children transformed into shrieks of rage. They came to a stop just outside and screamed at him. Wordless sounds full of a deep and chilling hatred.

"Watch your eyes," John said, his voice coming from the left in the utter darkness of the crypt.

Brian closed them.

There was a roll and a snap and John said, "Okay."

When Brian looked, he saw John held a lighter above his head. It cast a small circle of light and as John turned, it illuminated an old flashlight the size of a car battery as well as a hurricane lamp. The items stood on a small shelf cut into the earthen wall.

Brian brushed some webs off the flashlight, hit the switch and was pleased to see it spray light across the crypt.

Although what it revealed quickly tempered his happiness. Row upon row of stone markers were set into the sides of the crypt. Hundreds of them. Each bore a number, and nothing more.

Brian saw that the ceiling was arched, cobwebs thick in the barely penetrated darkness. At the far end of the flashlight's range, he caught sight of a second door. It was smaller, much smaller than the one which they had entered. From what he could tell, it too, was made of iron.

The air around them was heavy and cold.

"I think we should get to the second door, sooner rather than later," John whispered.

Brian nodded.

John took the hurricane lamp and together they began to walk quickly towards the far end of the crypt.

They had gone no more than a dozen paces when Brian felt as though he was being watched.

A quick glance at the stone doors of the burial niches revealed it to be true.

Faces peered out of the stone. Some of them were confused. Others angry. None of them looked especially pleased to see either Brian or John. Brian didn't want to find out why, or what the dead would do about it. He had a suspicion it wouldn't be good.

"Got the key?" John asked in a low voice.

"Yeah," Brian answered, keeping his own voice barely above a whisper. He had the key ready.

Hands appeared. They reached out of the stone doors to grasp the edges. Slowly, almost casually, the ghosts began to pull themselves out.

Whispers filled the air.

"…see you…"

"…smell you…"

"…are you afraid?"

And more words and phrases he couldn't quite catch. The closer he and John drew to the second door, the louder the voices became.

The angrier their tones grew.

"Quick!" John hissed as they reached the iron barrier.

Brian kept the flashlight in one hand, and the weight of it made the muscles of his forearm scream in protest. He ignored them, slammed the key into the lock and turned it sharply. For a moment, it caught, and he had a flash of panic.

Did I break the key? Is the lock jammed? he wondered.

And then the door opened.

It swung into another room, and he and John hastened into it.

Brian pulled the key free, and John slammed the door back into place.

"Oh no," Brian said, shining his light around him.

"What?" John asked, turning around. "Oh! Oh, this isn't good at all."

Brian couldn't respond. He couldn't look away from the skeleton which lay on the floor before them.

CHAPTER 9

JENNY MAKES A CALL, 9:10 AM, MAY 2ND, 2016

When her boss, Anne, stepped out for a quick cigarette, Jenny picked up her phone and sent Brian a text. Nothing more than an emoticon with hearts for eyes and a swooning look.

A second after she hit 'send' the phone buzzed, she smiled, and looked down at it.

'Message Failed to Send.'

What? she asked herself. She hit send again, watched the screen, and saw the rejection come through, once more.

Bet it's the damned location, she thought. Jenny quickly navigated over to Google, found the number for the Woods Cemetery and dialed it.

The phone rang three times before it was picked up.

"Woods Cemetery, Joe speaking," an old man said.

"Hi Joe," Jenny said happily, "my husband, Brian, is supposed to be working there today. Is he around?"

"Brian?" Joe said. "Oh, Brian Roy. He's the new boss in town, right?"

"Yes," she said.

"Nice fella," Joe said cheerfully. "Well, he's speaking with a family right now. Would you like me to take a message and ask him to give you a callback?"

"You know, a callback would be great, Joe," Jenny said.

"Okay then, Mrs. Roy, I'll be sure to tell Brian you called," Joe said, and he sounded like the sweetest old man on the face of the planet.

"Great, thanks!"

"You're welcome," Joe said pleasantly, and he hung up the phone.

She would give Brian another call, or send him a text at lunchtime. She still had some paperwork to catch up on. Not to mention a ton of emails.

She put her phone down on the desk, logged into her work account and thought, *I'll have to make sure and tell Brian what a nice man Joe is. He was really helpful and pleasant.*

Jenny hummed to herself as she scanned her emails and looked for anything which could possibly be construed as important.

CHAPTER 10

BRIAN AND JOHN IN THE CRYPT, 9:10 AM, MAY 2ND, 2016

While Jenny had an exceptionally pleasant conversation with a man named Joe, Brian and John looked at the skeletal remains in front of them.

"He," John said, setting the hurricane lamp down on the stone floor, "does not look like he came out on top of anything."

"Definitely not," Brian said. Behind him, he could hear the voices, their words lost on the other side of the iron door.

John walked forward, knelt down and looked closer at the skeleton.

It wore clothes dusty from years of solitude. The skeleton was once a man, and he had been dressed in a pair of jeans, black work boots, and a red sweater. A silver ring remained on the index finger of the left hand, and a pair of horn-rimmed glasses rested on his chest. The arms of the frames were connected by the fine links of a silver chain.

John, with exceptional care, searched the man's pockets. A few moments later, he was rewarded with the discovery of a wallet.

"What's this?" John asked in a soft voice, which Brian suspected was more for John's own benefit than his. John reached behind the body and carefully removed a small satchel. He scooted away from the body and motioned for Brian to join him, and Brian did.

The floor was cold and uncomfortable, but it felt good to sit down. Brian felt adrenaline drain into his stomach. And even though Brian knew the biochemical process, what it meant and the purpose it served, it didn't make him feel any less nauseous.

Brian realized, painfully, how he and John were trapped in the crypt. Within the cemetery. By the fence and the fog. And in spite of his ability to see and converse with the dead, regardless of his previous experiences, Brian was completely and utterly subservient to the situation.

He hated it.

"You okay?" John asked as Brian adjusted his position.

"Scared," Brian said truthfully, "and frustrated. I know what ghosts can do. Scares the hell out of me."

"Well, maybe one of these will be our lucky door," John said, gesturing around the room.

For the first time, Brian really took note of their small prison. It was circular, with the iron entrance behind them and half a dozen more doors in the curved walls. Each lintel was labeled with a Roman numeral, one through six, the brass secured firmly to the wide planks. The doors were painted a dark green and were narrow and short.

Brian's skin crawled as he looked at them.

They lead to nothing good, Brian thought. *Only variations of bad, and each worse than the one before it.*

"They don't feel right," John said softly.

"No," Brian agreed. "Definitely not. Do you want to open up the wallet and see who our roommate was?"

John nodded, set the old satchel on his lap and opened up the wallet. It contained an assortment of color pictures kept in a cracked plastic accordion sleeve, fifteen dollars in singles, some random scraps of paper with short sentences like, 'the oak on Elm,' and 'Fire on Mulberry.'

John found the license tucked behind a YMCA membership card. The picture on the license was of a young man. Dusty blonde hair fell to the shoulders and rested easily on the plaid shirt he wore. His face was wide and open, and he had a smirk.

"Mitchell Farmington," John read. "Age twenty-two, born April first, 1960."

"He's been here a long time," Brian said after a moment of silence.

"Yeah," John agreed. He returned everything to the wallet and placed it on Mitchell's chest.

"Think he might have written something down?" Brian asked, motioning towards the satchel.

"Hm? Maybe, we should check it out," John said absently. "Let's light the hurricane lamp, though. Save some of the battery's juice in the flashlight."

"Sounds good," Brian said. He passed the lamp over to John, and the man took out his lighter. He raised the shade, adjusted the wick, and then he lit it.

The flame from the lamp was strong and burned a bright blue just below the orange tip. John lowered the shade, and Brian turned off the flashlight. It was best to save it for later, and Brian hoped like hell there was going to be a *later*.

A whole lot of *later*.

John put his lighter away, turned the wick up a little higher for more light, and then turned his attention to the satchel.

Brian watched the older man work at the straps and the buckles, which were green with age. John finally freed the straps and left smears of cleared space on the leather. He wiped off the dust and grime on his pants and glanced over at Brian then smiled.

"Well," John said, "let's see what Mitchell had brought with him."

The leather flap hissed and creaked as John pushed it up and back. From the narrow depths of the satchel, he removed a pair of black and white composition notebooks, several pens, an old Hershey's chocolate bar wrapper, and a bottle of Coke. John set them all out on the floor between them and Mitchell.

The notebooks looked remarkably untouched by their thirty plus years in the room.

"Would you like to do the honors?" John asked.

"I would love to," Brian said. He reached out and picked up one of the notebooks and opened it. Page after page of free verse poetry, most of it about life in a small city. The penmanship was neat, mistakes crossed out, and the corrections jotted above them.

Brian flipped through the entire notebook, shook his head and set it down. "Poetry."

John nodded and handed Brian the second notebook.

The first few pages were filled with poems, but afterward, the pages were filled with word after word after word.

The opening line stated,

I am trapped…

CHAPTER 11

MITCHELL'S NOTEBOOK, PART ONE, MAY 4TH, 1980

I am trapped.

I am still not quite certain what happened, or how I ended up here. It is all a terrible dream. A nightmare from which I cannot awaken.

It began in a common enough way, and I suppose the banality of its beginning is part of the horror.

I decided to walk from my room on Washington Street to Woods. The cemetery is always a source of inspiration for me. A place to think and consider life; a sanctuary in which to reflect.

I brought my notebooks; the first one, I knew I would finish with since I had only a few pages. I brought pens in case one went dry.

The morning was fine. A beautiful spring morning. I went and sat by the Greeley's plot, the elm tree there offering shade. I wrote steadily for an hour or so. I filled the last of one notebook and had started the second. When I finally paused to stretch, I saw a fog had rolled in.

It was a strange and curious fog. Thicker than any I had seen before, except for those on the beaches of Maine. I assumed the marshes, nearby, were responsible for it. I prepared to return to my writing when I saw how the fog followed the fence line and did not pass it. It was as though I was wrapped in a cocoon.

And at first, it was a pleasant and comfortable feeling.

The cemetery had always been a place of rest and safety. Why would I be afraid of a bit of fog?

I should have been.

Instead of returning to my writing, I should have left, fled, run from the place. Yet foolishly, I continued to write, to work on my craft. It will cost me my life, I am afraid.

No sooner had I begun a new poem, then I heard laughter. When I looked up, I saw a young woman on the cemetery road. She was tall and thin, and she wore a faded yellow wedding dress.

I thought it rather odd and I worried for a moment, whether or not she was mentally stable.

Only for a moment, though, for then I realized her skin was a deathly white. Vicious, like a cold, hard snow. Her eyes were black. Not only her pupils and irises but the whites as well. The entire orb was black, and her eyes were locked on mine.

When she saw me look at her, she threw her head back and let loose a laugh. The sound was so raw, so vile it caused my hands to shake.

I threw my notebooks back into my satchel and got to my feet. I turned to flee and saw half a dozen others. They stood before the gate, each with a terrible smile. Some had gray skin, while others were almost alabaster white. Each had black eyes, though, and I knew they sought my death.

And I knew, deep within, how my soul would suffer if they slew me.

I ran and searched for a place to hide. If you are reading this, then you, whoever you are, have found my hiding place.

My prison.

My grave.

I suffer no illusions about whether or not I shall escape from here.

He has told me this is my place of dying.

The owner of the voice, the man who spoke to me, who urged me to hide as the dead chased me through the cemetery. I have not seen this man. I know I shall soon.

I hope, if you are trapped here with my remains, I can be of some assistance. I have traveled through all six of these doors, and I can tell you what to expect within each.

None of them, let me assure you, lead to freedom, safety, or life. My return to this ante-chamber is nothing short of a miracle.

Danger sits like a fat and swollen spider in its web, waiting for the unwary.

Say a prayer for me, and I wish for you a quick death, and not the lingering starvation which I am sure is my fate.

CHAPTER 12

PICKING A DOOR, 9:30 AM, MAY 2ND, 2016

"Do you mind if I smoke?" John asked.

Brian shook his head. "Light up, John. Light up."

John shook out a cigarette, placed it between his lips and lit it. Once he had exhaled the first drag, he looked from Mitchell to the notebook and finally to Brian.

"So, the papers from the office, they said we had to hide as best we could?" he asked.

"Yes," Brian said. "And Mitchell here, told us there's danger behind every door."

"But we're going to have to pick one to go through," John said. He glanced at the iron entrance. "And they'll get through, soon enough?"

"So the papers say," Brian said, sighing. "I know the iron will hold them off directly, but they must know of another way in. I don't hear them on the other side."

John cocked his head, listened for a moment and then nodded. "True. Looks like we've got to play ourselves one hell of a game of hide and seek."

Brian chuckled bitterly. "Sounds about right."

John looked back at the six doors.

"Guess we'll have to read about Mitchell's experiences?" John asked.

"More than likely," Brian said. He stared past John and at the six choices before them. "I really just want to know why this is happening."

"Trying not to think about the why of it," John said momentarily.

Brian looked over at him and frowned. "Why not?"

"Just going to take up time, make me a little more worried," John explained. "We can't really afford either of those, can we?"

Brian shook his head. "No. No, I suppose we can't."

Brian looked down at the notebook, and then he jerked his head up sharply.

"What is it?" John asked in a low voice, taking his cigarette out of his mouth.

Brian held up a finger, cocked his head to one side and closed his eyes. John closed his eyes too, and listened.

He heard the rapid beat of his heart, the exhalation of air through his nose and the inhalation through his mouth. He felt the cold and the raw edge of fear which chewed at his confidence and threatened to overwhelm him. He smelled the musky odor of death and a bitter hint of sorrow.

And then he heard it.

A light, insistent scratching. Coming from one of the wooden doors.

With a shudder, John opened his eyes and saw Brian had done the same. The younger man pointed to the third door, and John nodded.

The scratching came from the door's center. As John listened, he could hear the sound move down slowly, ever so slowly to the bottom. Suddenly, the scratches stopped.

Then a dark gray finger appeared. The nail was like polished obsidian. It caught the light of hurricane lamp, took it in, turned it around and let it glow dully. A second finger, and then a third and a fourth joined it. Finally, the thumb made an appearance and the entire hand was present and accounted for. It would slide in, palm down, and then slip out only to return a second later with the palm up. It rattled the door, pulled at it, and then it focused on the floor.

It wasn't the hands insistence, or the color of the flesh or the darkness of the nail which bothered John, though. It wasn't the smell or the sight of it which caused a hitch in his breath or the knot in his stomach.

It was the hand's size; tiny, no larger than a toddler's.

Yet the malignant nature of it numbed John's mind as surely as the touch of another had damaged his flesh with cold.

And then he heard more scratches from the doors on either side of number three.

They've sent the children in first, John realized, horrified. *The children. Small enough to get in first and open a door for the others. For something worse.*

"Come on," Brian said, his voice raw with fear. "Looks like door number one is the winner for today."

John merely stood up, held onto the hurricane lamp and waited or Brian to gather up the flashlight and Mitchell's notes on the doors.

Without a word, Brian walked to door number one, took hold of the wooden latch and led the way out of the chamber.

John followed as quickly as he could.

CHAPTER 13

DOOR NUMBER ONE, 9:35 AM, MAY 2ND, 2016

When the door closed behind them, Brian felt fear settle into the back of his mind.

This is a bad situation, he told himself. *And this, this isn't helping things at all.*

He and John stood in a small corridor, perhaps twenty feet long with walls close to his shoulders. If he went up on his tiptoes, he would hit his head on the ceiling. The entire length was made of old red bricks. The mortar was shrunken and crumbled in some places. And the only light was cast by the lamp. The end of the corridor looked to be a sharp turn, but until they got closer, Brian wouldn't be able to tell.

He put the flashlight down on the floor between his feet and opened up the notebook. By the lamp's dim light, he found and read Mitchell's section about the first door aloud,

> *"There is no way to differentiate or to grade the horrors behind each door. I can only catalog them. The first door opens to a corridor which leads to a larger passage and two rooms. These rooms are the home of a man who has been dead for a long time. He is brutal and wicked, and delights in torture. I don't think I escaped his clutches. I think he let me go so I might experience other horrors, and die of slow starvation. His name, I believe, is Malachi, and he would make the greatest of inquisitors seem like nothing more than amateurs."*

"Well," John said with a sigh, "I can't say I find this particularly encouraging."

"Neither do I," Brian agreed. He closed the notebook and picked up the flashlight. "Let's see what we can do."

"Lead on," John said.

Brian did so. His heart fluttered nervously within his chest.

Christ I don't want to die down here, he thought. The reality of it weighed heavily upon him.

Within a few moments, they reached the end of the corridor and found it turned to the left and spread out considerably. The walls were still made of brick, as was the ceiling and the floor. On the left, was a single door made of wood and painted a dark blue. On the right, was one identical to it.

Brian took a few steps into the new chamber and came to a stop. John did the same and kept within arm's distance of him. Pressure began to build in Brian's head. The sensation was decidedly unpleasant and soon bordered on painful. It felt as though someone was behind each eye and sought to push them out of the sockets. For a moment, Brian had a mental image of his eyes dangling from their optic nerves and resting on his cheeks.

"Jesus," John hissed. "Get out of my head!"

Brian couldn't even speak, his tongue had swollen in his mouth, and he found it impossible to speak.

A harsh laugh filled the chamber and changed to sharp snarl.

"How do you like it?" John spat.

The pain vanished from Brian, and he looked at John.

The man's face was a mask of rage. "You don't like it do you? No, I know you don't. Let me in and I'll pump you so full of pain, you'll wish you were deader than you are now."

"Silence!" a man snarled, and a moment later, a shape stepped out of the far brick wall.

CHAPTER 14

THE CONTEST, 9:40 AM, MAY 2ND, 2016

John stood there, angry. He was filled with a rage he hadn't felt since Vietnam.

And he had been angry when he was in the jungle. Especially after he'd been hit with the Molotov cocktail.

Somehow, he was able to send it back to the ghost which sought to hurt him. Which had sent the pain into his head. John felt as though there was a path between himself and the torturer, and he fed all of it back, tenfold.

The pain in his head vanished.

John took a step forward and looked at the dead man who had walked through the wall and into the room.

The man wore a set of clothes which looked like the Puritans could have brought them over from England. He was tall and thin, his skin the darkest gray that John had ever seen. The eyes didn't even look black so much as they did empty.

"Malachi," John said, setting the hurricane lamp on the floor.

For a moment, Malachi looked surprised. The expression vanished quickly.

"You know my name," the ghost said.

"Seems like it's the most impressive part about you," John said.

"I'll teach you to keep a civil tongue in your head," Malachi said softly. "Or I'll have it out of your mouth altogether."

John chuckled. "Pretty good little speech there, Malory."

"Malachi," the ghost said, anger creeping into his voice.

"Melinda?" John asked innocently.

"Malachi!" the dead man shouted.

"Michelle?" John said, taking a short step forward.

"*Malachi!* You stupid, ignorant fool!" Malachi shrieked.

John felt the ghost's anger wash over him, push at him, and John brought up all of his memories of being wounded. The pain, the fear. John threw it all at Malachi and watched with satisfaction as the ghost took a step backward.

Malachi dropped down to a knee, head bent. "No."

Brian groaned beside John, and he glanced at the man. Brian's eyes were shut tightly, perspiration on his head.

John's rage flared up, and he focused it on Malachi again.

This time, Malachi screamed and fell onto the floor.

John looked at the dead man, who rolled onto his back and gasped as he stared up at the ceiling.

"Are you alright?" John asked, looking at Brian.

Brian nodded, his face pale. "Felt like he reached in and squeezed my heart. Not the best thing for me."

"Not the best for anyone," John said. "Be right back."

John walked forward to where the ghost lay and squatted down next to him. Malachi smelled of a dead animal. The stench of a big raccoon who'd been hit on the highway and had spent weeks there.

The black depths of Malachi's eyes rolled to fix upon John. "Who are you?"

"Me?" John asked, surprised. "I'm just a man."

"Your face," Malachi said.

"Fire," John replied. "Terrible fire. You should see my chest."

"The pain," Malachi said, shuddering. "I have never known it."

"Now you have," John said, and he knew he had a weapon against the dead man. "Now, I don't suppose you'll tell us how to leave the cemetery?"

"Leave?" Malachi asked. He chuckled. "Oh no. There is no leaving, my new friend. If He lets you go, then you shall leave. Until then, you are His guest. Nothing more. Nothing less. Survive in here as long as you can. If He is impressed, He will let you leave. If not, well then, we'll have more time to get acquainted."

"Best way out of here?" John asked.

Malachi smiled. A wicked smile of crooked, yellow teeth.

At the far wall, a door made of bricks swung into the room.

"Travel carefully," Malachi warned. "There are far worse residents than myself in the crypt."

Before John could ask who they might be, Malachi sank down into the floor and vanished.

John looked back at Brian and smiled. "Looks like we'll take the new door."

Brian gave a weak grin. "Sound good to me."

CHAPTER 15

JENNY STARTS TO GET CONCERNED, 9:40 AM, MAY 2ND, 2016

Jenny picked up her cellphone again and checked the volume on the alerts. Brian still hadn't called or texted her. Her own text still hadn't gone through.

She picked up the office phone and called the cemetery again. After two rings, it was answered. She recognized the voice.

"Hi Joe," she said. "Is Brian there?"

Joe chuckled. "No. Well, yes and no. Does that help?"

Jenny shook her head. "No, it doesn't help. Can I speak with my husband, please?"

"He can't be reached by phone right now," Joe said pleasantly.

"Is he still talking with some people?" she asked.

"No," Joe said. "He's trapped in the crypt."

Jenny felt cold suddenly. "What? What do you mean?"

"Brian has quite the reputation amongst the dead, Mrs. Roy," Joe said, his voice becoming harsh and angry. A note of power ran through his words and Jenny's throat tightened.

"Who are you?" she asked softly.

"Someone who feels privileged to have Brian here," Joe said, chuckling. "I wish to see how well he can do. A few others have survived this, so there is a chance he might as well. Of course, none of them had such troublesome hearts."

"Why?" she whispered. "Why are you doing this?"

"Why?" Joe asked, sounding surprised. "Well, perhaps a better question is why not? I have been dead a very, very long time. I am bored; he is entertaining."

"What if something happens to him?" Jenny asked.

"You'll know where to bring the flowers," Joe said, and he hung up.

Jenny tried to call back, but she only received a busy signal. She returned the phone to the cradle, stood up and went to tell Anne she was going home sick.

Chapter 16
Traveling through the Unknown, 9:40 am, May 2nd, 2016

Brian walked slowly. He listened to his heart, made sure the rhythm was steady. Malachi's cardiac squeeze had nearly done him in.

Brian glanced at John. The older man had taken the lead and lighted the way as they traveled along a corridor fashioned from stones, wooden timbers, and packed earth. It felt as though they walked on a downward slope. The air remained chilly and harsh. A glance at his phone had shown he was still out of service, and the time was only twenty to ten, in the morning.

It felt as though hours, not minutes, had passed.

Brian was exhausted, hungry, and tired.

But there would be no rest.

No rest for the wicked, he thought, smiling to himself. *And you have been wicked. I don't know if I've deserved this, though.*

"How are you feeling?" John asked, glancing back at him.

Brian shook his head. "You know the first day when you reach basic training, and you realize you made the worst mistake of your life?"

John chuckled. "Yeah?"

"Yeah, just like it," Brian said, sighing.

"Understood," John said. "Let me know if you need me to carry the flashlight. Thing looks like it weighs a ton."

"Thanks," Brian said, "I'll swing it for now."

"Fair enough," John said.

The passage curved gently to the left, and when it straightened out again, a round door which reminded Brian of Bilbo Baggins, stood before them.

Pretty sure there's no happy little hobbit in there, though, Brian thought.

John hissed and stumbled.

Brian reached out, caught the man by his arm and asked, "Are you okay?"

For a moment, John didn't answer, and when he finally did, his voice was filled with pain. "My leg. Where the ghost had grabbed me earlier. Felt like someone just drove a bunch of needles into it."

"Let me take a look," Brian said, turning on the flashlight. He aimed the beam at John's leg as the man pulled up the pants.

"Damn," Brian whispered.

When he had seen the injury in the office, the frostbite had covered about a hand's width of flesh. Now the skin had a blotchy black and gray appearance, and stretched from the brown sock John wore and up to the knee.

John looked down, saw it, and whistled between his teeth. He dropped the pants leg, winced as the fabric brushed the skin, and gave Brian a grim smile.

"Doesn't look too good, now does it," he said.

Brian shook his head. "No, John, it looks pretty damned bad."

"Probably why it hurts so much," John said.

"Probably," Brian replied. He turned off the light. There was nothing he could do about the leg. The best chance John had was to get out of the cemetery and get to a doctor. Brian didn't even have a knife he could use to amputate the leg if it came to it, and no matter how tough John was, Brian doubted the man could handle a surgery without some sort of anesthetic.

And why would he want to? Brian asked himself.

"Ready for door number two?" John asked, interrupting Brian's train of thoughts.

"Of course not," Brian said. "But we don't have much of a choice."

"No," John agreed, "we don't. Want to do the honors?"

"Sure," Brian said. He stepped forward, took hold of a brass knob and revealed the next challenge.

The room looked normal. Almost like someone's living room or library. Four large bookcases occupied the left wall, each shelf filled with books of various sizes and colors. A long, dark wood desk stood in the center of the right wall. An easy chair with a floor lamp was at the far wall. Several jackets hung on pegs on the right of the door, and a porcelain and brass chandelier hung from the ceiling. Warm, pleasant light fell from the candle shaped bulbs, and the room smelled of fresh coffee.

Brian didn't trust any of it.

When both he and John stepped into the room, the door closed and locked.

Brian waited for the chandelier to go out, but it remained lit. He looked over at John, who shrugged.

They had stood for nearly a minute before Brian took a cautious step forward.

The ceiling stretched a little. The effect was instant, he felt queasy and disorientated.

John moved to the left, and the air grew heavy, difficult to breathe.

A man appeared in the chair. He wore a red sweater and a pair of jeans. The work boots on his feet were black, and he had silver framed, horn-rimmed glasses on his face. A silver ring on his index finger reflected the light of the chandelier. The man's skin was the deathly pale white Brian had seen on a few other ghosts, and his eyes were the same black. His hair was dusty blonde, and it fell just past the shoulders. He flashed Brian and John a wicked grin.

John took a half a step forward, and a bitter cold swept over them.

Brian shivered so violently he dropped the notebook and the flashlight. He thrust his hands under his arms and winced as the cold acted like a vise and squeezed his temples.

The dead man's grin widened and Brian straightened up.

"Mitchell?" Brian asked.

The grin faltered.

The cold vanished.

"Mitchell Farmington," Brian said.

Suddenly the air was no longer heavy.

"You're the poet," John said.

The room snapped into normalcy.

Mitchell looked at them, confused. Then, in a deep, strong voice he asked, "How do you know me?"

Brian moved cautiously and slowly bent down. He picked up the dropped notebook and held it up for Mitchell to see.

"My notebook," Mitchell said softly, his eyes locked on it. After a moment, he looked to Brian and said, "You found my notebook."

"Both of them," Brian said. "But we only brought this one. We hoped to use your information to escape from here. Would you like it back?"

Mitchell nodded.

Brian took several slow steps forward and then he handed it to the ghost. An electric shock rippled through the cardboard and paper to race along Brian's flesh. He let go and went back to stand with John.

Mitchell looked at the notebook for a moment before he opened it. He adjusted his glasses, read a page, smiled, and read another. With a sigh, he closed the notebook and held onto it. He took his glasses off and let them hang from their chain against his chest.

"I was promised," he said, "the right to kill whomever stumbled into my room. I did not hope for it to happen, for who would have been able to pass by Malachi? Would I ever obtain some sort of revenge upon the world for my death?"

Neither Brian nor John answered.

"And when some semblance of joy has been delivered to me, they carry my own words with them." Mitchell shook his head. He smiled sadly at them. "May I help you in some way, gentlemen?"

"Is there a way out?" John asked.

Mitchell hesitated, and then he nodded. "It is difficult. Leave by the door you came, and do your best. I can say no more about it."

"Did you ever find out who it was?" Brian asked.

Mitchell frowned.

"The man, the one who trapped you here," Brian pressed.

Mitchell's eyes widened, and he whispered, "Yes."

"Who?" Brian asked. "Who is it?"

"Names are power," Mitchell hissed.

"Please," Brian implored.

Mitchell hesitated for only a moment before he whispered, "Josephus Wahlen."

CHAPTER 17

OUT THROUGH THE IN DOOR, 9:50 AM, MAY 2ND, 2016

When Brian looked for the circular door they had entered, it was no longer there. Slightly to the left of, where it had been, was a short, rectangular door. With trepidation, Brian led the way out.

They stepped into a room which spread out before them. It was a darkened ballroom, with half a dozen crystal chandeliers. Corinthian pillars stood at intervals along the walls, and between each pair was a tall window with floor-length draperies. The floor glowed with a high polish. The room was as cold as any of the others through which Brian and John had passed. At the corners the light of John's hurricane lamp was absorbed, each a darkness too strong for any illumination to penetrate.

At the far end of the ballroom, a trio of doors stood. They were tall, wide, and white paneled. The knobs looked to be cut crystal, and they matched the chandeliers. The room spoke of elegance and beauty, and stank of death and fear.

Brian was not surprised when the circular door closed and locked behind them of its own accord.

"I have to say," John said, "I am not enjoying this little exploration of ours."

"Makes two of us, my friend," Brian said. He shifted the flashlight from one hand to the other. "I've dealt with some strange stuff before, but this beats all of them."

"Glad to know it's not just me who thinks this whole situation is odd," John said.

"How's your leg?" Brian asked.

"Bad," John grunted. He looked at Brian. "I've got no illusions here, Brian. Whatever hurt me wasn't natural, and the injury isn't either. I suspect it'll kill me before long. My only goal is to not die here. I'd like to make it out, have Emily exhumed and put in a plot where her spirit won't be trapped."

"Understood," Brian said.

"If I do die here, though," John said somberly, "will you try and have her moved? I doubt you'll be able to bring me, too, but at least get her out?"

Brian nodded. He had seen John's leg and knew it was a death sentence in the crypt.

"Thank you," John said. He looked back to the doors at the end of the ballroom. "Looks like we have another choice in front of us."

"Reminds me of some books I used to read as a kid," Brian said, chuckling. "Those 'Choose Your Own Adventure' ones."

John laughed. "Hey, I had a nephew who loved those books. He tried to explain them to me once, didn't quite see the enjoyment in them."

"I think you had to be a kid," Brian said, and then he sighed. "Ready?"

"Not at all," John replied. He shrugged his shoulders and said, "We don't have a choice, though, other than the door we go through. Any particular choice?"

Brian looked at the identical doors.

His gut twisted into a tighter knot.

Brian shook his head. "They're all bad."

"Agreed," John said. "Might as well try this door."

"Lead on, my friend, lead on," Brian said, gesturing towards the far end.

John did so, and Brian followed.

As they walked the floor stretched out, the room grew longer.

It felt as though they were on an escalator and going nowhere.

John glanced from right to left and shook his head. "I'm pretty sure rooms aren't supposed to do this."

"Agreed," Brian said, "but the dead aren't supposed to pull themselves out of their headstones and attack us, either."

John chuckled. "Very true."

When they stopped in front of the far wall, Brian looked back. The ballroom was now the length of a football field, the round entrance to

Mitchell's chamber now difficult to see.

He fought back a shudder and returned his attention to the right door.

John looked at him with fear and caution in his eyes.

Brian swallowed nervously, cleared his throat and nodded.

John took hold of the crystal knob, turned it and revealed the next horror.

CHAPTER 18

JENNY VISITS WOODS CEMETERY, 10:15 AM, MAY 2ND, 2016

Jenny broke a considerable number of motor vehicle rules on her way back to Mont Vernon.

Part of her was impressed with her luck. In spite of her excessive speed, or how she ignored traffic lights and road signs, no one had pulled her over.

When she reached the cemetery, she slammed on the brakes. With her hands tight upon the steering wheel, she stared in shock at what was in front of her.

A wall of fog.

It was *massive*.

The fog stretched up and into a low, dark cloud which seemed to threaten something far worse than a shower or burst of rain. The fence was hidden from her view, as was any part of the cemetery.

Brian was in the cemetery, with someone named Joe. Joe, who seemed intent upon doing something sinister to Brian.

Jenny took her foot off the brake, pulled over onto the side of the road and shut the engine down. She tucked the keys under the floor mat and got out of the car. She left the doors unlocked and walked up to the where the entrance of the cemetery should be.

With a deep breath, Jenny forced herself to calm down, to remember what the entrance had looked like. The image came quickly. The granite pillars, the wrought iron fence. The office off to the right.

She opened her eyes and walked forward.

Her feet struck the pavement. Each step on the hard surface reassured her of the reality of it.

And she walked into the fog.

It wrapped around her, thick and cold. Bitterly cold. It set her teeth to rattling and her bones to aching. Jenny balled her hands into fists and continued on. The fog muffled the world, and her heartbeat became painfully loud in her ears.

A soft voice came out of the fog. "Who are you?"

The speaker was young, either a boy or a girl, Jenny couldn't be sure which.

"My name's Jenny," she replied. "What's yours?"

The speaker hesitated a moment. "My name is Ruth."

"Why aren't you in school, Ruth?" Jenny asked. She looked around and tried to see the girl. "Are you home schooled?"

"No," Ruth said, the voice coming closer. "I'm dead."

Oh Jesus, really? Jenny thought.

"Are you buried here?" Jenny asked.

"In the fog?" Ruth said.

Jenny made out a small form off to her left, and she kept her eyes upon it.

"No," Jenny said. "No, not the fog. Here, in the cemetery."

"No," Ruth said after a moment. "I am not buried in the cemetery. And you're not in the cemetery."

"What?" Jenny asked, looking down at her feet. Between her shoes, she could see asphalt. "Where am I then?"

"You're in the fog," Ruth replied. "And the fog doesn't let people into the cemetery."

"How do I get into the cemetery?" Jenny asked.

"You have to wait until He lets you in," Ruth said.

"Who?"

"Josephus," Ruth whispered. "Only He can make the fog part. But He never does."

"Are you trapped in the fog, Ruth?" Jenny asked, wondering if perhaps the girl knew a way around Josephus.

"No," Ruth said. "I live here."

"Are there others?" Jenny said.

"A few," Ruth said. She stepped closer and Jenny saw her for the first time.

Ruth was perhaps ten or eleven, and she wore a pair of denim overalls with white and black saddle shoes. She was a pretty little girl, her dark brown hair pulled up into pigtails. Her big eyes were a light blue, and her nose was small. She smiled at Jenny and Jenny saw the bottom teeth were crowded together as if she had too many of them.

Jenny returned the smile. "Hello, Ruth."

"Hi," Ruth said, putting her hands into her pockets.

"Is there any way you can lead me into the cemetery?" Jenny asked.

Ruth shook her head sadly. "Only Josephus can let people in. Or out. He never lets me out."

Jenny frowned. "What happened to you?"

"To me?" Ruth asked with a smile. "No one ever asks. They're usually too afraid. But do you really want to know?"

"Yes, please," Jenny said.

"Well," Ruth said, "I came with Mr. Butterman, from the music store. He said he wanted to show me something special, down in the back."

Jenny repressed a shudder and kept her smile on her face. She was sure Mr. Butterman hadn't had anything nice to show the girl.

"I didn't get to see it, though," Ruth said sadly. "We had just gotten to the back by the crypt, and Mr. Butterman had set up a picnic. He even had *wine*. He was going to let me drink some, like a grown up."

I bet, Jenny thought. Yet she kept smiling.

"We had just started to eat, and then these ghosts came out of the headstones, and the only place to hide was the crypt. It was unlocked for some reason, and Mr. Butterman and I ran in there.

"We got to another room and a bunch of doors, and we ran, and we ran. Ghosts were everywhere!" Ruth said excitedly. "Then, something bad happened."

"What?" Jenny asked.

"We met a monster. A great, big monster and it killed Mr. Butterman," Ruth said in a low voice. "It killed him dead."

"Did it kill you, too?" Jenny asked.

Ruth shook her head. "It left me alone. And I died there, next to Mr. Butterman. He's an angry, angry ghost."

"He is?" Jenny said. "Why?"

"He says he's angry because he didn't get to show me the special surprise," Ruth said, smiling. "And he's angry about what I did."

"What did you do?" Jenny asked.

"I ate him," Ruth said, reaching up and playing with a loose curl of her hair. "I was *so* hungry. There was nothing else to eat, so one of the ghosts who lives here told me to. She said it was okay."

"Oh," Jenny said softly.

Ruth nodded. "Right down to the bone. I think he's pretty upset about it."

Jenny was about to commiserate with her when Ruth's eyes went wide.

"What's wrong?" Jenny asked, looking around. "What is it?"

Ruth looked around wildly and took a nervous step closer to Jenny. "Don't you hear Him? Can't you *smell* Him?"

Jenny strained her ears, yet she heard nothing.

But when she inhaled deeply through her nose she could smell something. A terrible, sickening scent. She gagged and looked around as she clutched her hands to her stomach. Her throat hurt and clenched spasmodically.

Foul wasn't a strong enough word to describe the smell, it was beyond foul or wretched. It was as though someone had bottled the essence of putrid flesh and malignancy, and then released it into the air.

"You smell Him now, don't you?" Ruth asked.

Jenny nodded and whispered, "Who is it?"

"Josephus," Ruth whispered. "He's coming."

The cold deepened and Jenny's muscles tensed.

"Follow me," Ruth whispered and turned away.

Jenny did.

Ruth moved quickly, as though there was a path in the fog only she could see. The pavement beneath Jenny's feet shifted to grass, and her low heels were tugged at by the grass. The cold continued to follow and settled into her back. Jenny tried to ignore it, yet the fear in her continued to grow.

Ruth began to run, and so did Jenny.

"Where are you going, Jennifer?" a voice asked from behind her, and Jenny recognized it from the phone.

She knew it was Josephus, and he meant her harm.

"Straight ahead!" Ruth hissed. "Run!"

Jenny broke into a sprint, and a moment later, she broke free of the fog and stood in the morning's sun. She came to a stop and saw she stood half a dozen feet from her car. Jenny dropped to her knees, vomited, and began to weep.

Brian was in the cemetery and trapped in the fog.

CHAPTER 19

NOT ALONE, 10:20 AM, MAY 2ND, 2016

The room stank. A rank, foul stench of filth, rot and sorrow.

Brian nearly gagged on it, staggering back. The room discovered was rectangular, occupied by a large, dining table made from a rich, ebony wood with a dozen matching side chairs. The table was set with bright white dishes. Empty glasses and neatly folded cloth napkins of dark red, flanked each plate. Gleaming silverware spread out on either side; three forks of varying sizes on the left, a knife and two spoons on the right. Crystal and brass chandeliers hung from a vaulted ceiling. The room was bitterly cold, and what looked to be a dead man sat at the head of the table.

He was wrapped in a thick bearskin, his head leaning to the right. Long, thin hair hung in ropy strands to his chest. His sunken face was pale. The teeth, visible between parted lips which were nothing more than hints upon the desiccated flesh.

A short way behind the body was an exit. A tall door, perhaps nine or even ten feet high, although it couldn't have been more than a foot wide. It looked to be made of porcelain, the light of chandeliers reflected brilliantly in its depths.

"This is terrible," Brian said, trying to breathe only through his mouth.

John nodded in agreement, letting go of the doorknob as he stepped further into the room.

Brian followed, and the door slammed shut, causing his heart to jump. He glanced back and was surprised to see there was no doorknob.

The only way out was through the door which stood behind the man.

Brian turned back to the table and stopped.

The body was looking at him. Bright blue eyes stared across plates and silverware. The man smiled, and Brian felt dread nestle in his heart.

"John," Brian managed to say.

John paused, looked at the man in the chair and stopped sharply.

"You're alive," the living corpse said.

John nodded and Brian said, "Yes."

"Strange." The man's mouth barely moved as he spoke. "What are your names?"

"Brian Roy," Brian said.

"I'm John."

Then John asked, "What is yours?"

The man blinked, was quiet for nearly a minute and then said, "Owen. Owen Nickerson."

"How long have you been here, Owen?" Brian asked.

Owen smiled, a hideous expression filled with desperation. "A fair question. It deserves an equally fair answer. Yet, I do not have one to give. The truth, Brian, is I do not know how long I have been here. Perhaps you will tell me what year it is?"

"Two thousand sixteen," Brian said.

Owen's smile faltered and fell away. "Well, I must say, it certainly doesn't feel like I've been here for sixty years. Apparently I have, though."

"How old are you?" John asked in a whisper.

"I was twenty-five when I came here, and it doesn't feel as though more than a year has passed," Owen replied. "Although, I am sure I look much worse for the wear, do I not?"

Brian and John could only nod.

Owen closed his eyes, chuckling. "Yes. Twenty-five."

"There's nothing to eat here," John said after a moment. "How are you living?"

"Oh, there's food, eventually," Owen said. "He feeds me. He likes to keep me alive, although, I do not know why."

"Who?" Brian asked.

"Joe," Owen said, smiling his death's head grin. "Yes, Joe. He makes sure I have enough to eat, just not enough to make me strong enough to escape. I don't suppose I even want to leave, not anymore."

"Who's Joe?" John asked, looking confused.

"Josephus," Owen said knowingly. "And it seems he brought you here as well. He generally doesn't bring along a pair, though. This is new. This is *different*."

Brian cleared his throat and asked, "How, exactly, is this different?"

"I'm not sure which one of you I should eat first," Owen replied.

CHAPTER 20
JENNY MAKES A DECISION, 10:30 AM, MAY 2ND, 2016

As Jenny walked away from the bizarre fog which separated her from Brian, her mind raced. The world was nothing more than a backdrop to her thoughts. She followed various lines of possible plans to fruitless dead-ends. By the time she reached her car, she had considered and discarded ten of them. When she unlocked the car door, she had latched onto an eleventh.

Jenny put the car into drive and headed towards Nashua.

Behind her, the fog dissipated.

CHAPTER 21

TIME STANDS STILL

Josephus Wahlen stood in the gray world which was his, and his alone.

There were others in it, of course. They feared him, though, which was as it should be. He smiled as he watched the woman leave.

The little one, named Ruth, had helped her evade him. Ruth's sole purpose was to entertain, and she continued to do so. She was afraid of him, yet not paralyzed by the fear. Her actions were unpredictable, and it excited him.

As he watched the woman leave, he felt certain she would return, soon.

With the faintest of thoughts, Josephus scattered the fog, sending tendrils of it shooting back along the ground to the marsh. He smiled as he thought of the marsh. When he had been imprisoned in the crypt, the vibrant life from the tall reeds, and still waters had fed him, sustained him as his hatred grew.

Josephus had lived long enough, hated strong enough in the crypt to leave his flesh before he died.

He turned away from the road and made his way through the cemetery to the crypt. The other dead scattered, averting their eyes to avoid his wrath.

Josephus whistled to himself and wondered if Brian and the other one had met Owen yet.

CHAPTER 22

A Knock at the Door,
11:00 AM, May 2nd, 2016

He studied the chessboard for several minutes and tried to ignore Carl's smirk.

"You're not helping me think," the other man said in German.

Carl's smirk changed into an innocent smile as he replied, "My young friend, I have no idea of what you are speaking."

"I'm sure," he replied.

The doorbell rang, and Carl looked up, surprised. "I did not know you were expecting company."

"I'm not," he said with a sigh. He stood up, left the game and the dead man then went out into the hall. He was still in a pair of pajama pants and a tee shirt, his feet were bare.

When he reached the front door, he stopped and called out, in English, "Who is it?"

"My name's Jenny Roy," a woman said. "My husband is Brian. I'm looking for someone named Shane."

Shane Ryan opened the door and saw an attractive, middle-aged woman, her face pale and her lips pressed tightly together. "I'm Shane. Is everything alright?"

She shook her head.

"Come in," Shane said, and he moved aside. She stepped quickly into the house, her eyes scanning over everything. Shane closed the door and said, "Why don't we go to the study."

He led the way and called out in German, "Carl, I have a guest."

When he entered the room, Carl was gone, although the chess game remained where it was with Shane's king still in check.

"Please," Shane said, "sit down."

Jenny nodded and took the seat so recently occupied by Carl. If a chair could be occupied by a ghost.

"Okay," Shane said, "tell me what's going on."

She quickly spoke to him about Woods Cemetery in Mont Vernon, of the fog, of the phone call with a ghost. Of Brian being trapped.

At the end, she said, "I need your help."

Shane nodded. "We'll have to figure out what to do. Do you have problems with ghosts, Jenny?"

"No, not all of the time," Jenny said. "Why?"

"I'm going to have to ask a few friends to assist us," Shane answered. "And not all of them are alive."

"Go for it," Jenny said. "I want my husband back, and I want him alive."

"My goal as well," Shane said. In German, he said, "Carl, can you hear me? If so, will you come to the study?"

The air to the left of the chess board shimmered, and Carl appeared. Jenny didn't react.

"Should I make myself known?" Carl asked in his native language.

"Please," Shane answered in the same.

Carl nodded, and his faint image solidified ever so slightly. He looked like a superimposed image on a photograph, there but not really, and if Shane squinted, he could make out the study wall behind the dead man, but Carl was present enough for Jenny to notice him.

Her eyes widened, and her hands tightened upon the arms of the chair.

"Jenny," Shane said, speaking gently, "this is a very good friend of mine, Carl Hesselschwerdt."

Carl inclined his head slightly and gave her a small smile.

Jenny smiled back and asked, "So, how does this work?"

"A good question," Shane said. To Carl, he said in German, "Her husband is a friend of mine. He is trapped in a graveyard, by a mist. Will you do me the kindness of asking the dark ones if they know anything about such a thing?"

"Of course," Carl replied, and then he vanished.

Jenny was startled for a moment, and then she looked at Shane. "He'll help?"

"He will certainly try," Shane said. "He's going to ask around. I guess that's the best way to put it."

"Sort of like a ghost network?" Jenny asked.

"I've got a small library upstairs, too. It's almost all military stuff, but I'll look a little deeper." He stopped as her eyes widened. "Jenny, what's wrong?"

"A ghost library," she said softly. She smiled, "A ghost library."

"You lost me," Shane said. "I don't have a ghost library."

"No," Jenny said, shaking her head. "But, I do."

"What?"

"Yes," she said. "It was this man's, Leo's, it was his place. It's downtown, here in Nashua."

"Leo?" Shane asked. "Is he a ghost, because I think we've met?"

"Yes, you have met. Brian told me how Leo helped you guys up in Rye," Jenny said, nodding.

She stood up. "I need to get there. I'm sorry."

"Hold on," Shane said, getting to his feet. "Hold on. Why don't we go down together? I can help you look. Is it a big place?"

Jenny grinned. "Huge."

CHAPTER 23
CHOOSING LOTS

Brian looked at Owen warily.

The skeletal thin man smiled gruesomely.

"This is bull," John said, taking a step towards the door.

"John," Brian started to say.

Before he could tell the man to stop though, Owen's bearskin robe parted slightly. The blue steel barrel of a pistol appeared, and the distinctive sound of the hammer being cocked filled the room.

John stopped.

"Very good," Owen said, his voice low and pleasant. "Now, gentlemen, we have ourselves and interesting situation. Well, interesting for me, at least. Usually, Joseph merely sends the smaller of God's creatures to me, and I feast upon them. Rarely do I enjoy a full meal, although there have been others I have eaten. Unwary folk, or unlucky, like yourselves.

"Never, as I have said," Owen continued, "has Josephus delivered two to me. Part of me wishes to shoot you both and to be done with it. Yet, I have had frightfully little entertainment over the years. I have occupied myself with remembering books I have read. Films, seen as a boy."

Owen chuckled, and Brian was surprised to see the pistol never wavered. Owen was much stronger than he appeared.

"Are either of you familiar with 'the custom of the sea'?" Owen asked.

Both Brian and John shook their heads.

"A shame," Owen said. "Well, let me enlighten you, then. You see, my uncle was a fisherman, a Gloucester man by birth and by trade. Fished the Grand Banks for cod. He told me all sorts of delightful stories. When he was drunk, however, those stories were a little darker."

A thin, bony hand slipped out from under Owen's bearskin, took up a glass and brought it to his lips. Although Owen took a sip, Brian saw the glass was empty.

"Refreshing," Owen murmured. He smiled. "Yes. Now, when my dear uncle drank, he spoke of things that most people do not. And one of those was what he called 'the custom of the sea.' It sounds charming, doesn't it?"

John said nothing, and Brian only nodded.

"Alas, it is not," Owen said with a sigh. "It is a veiled reference to cannibalism. It speaks of men adrift at sea and starving to death. The good of the many outweighs the rights of the one. A single man would be sacrificed in order to sustain his comrades. The decision was made through the drawing of lots. The shortest straw, as it were."

Owen looked at Brian and John with his deathly grin.

"Jesus Christ," John hissed. "You can't be serious."

"I am," Owen said with feigned innocence. "I believe in fairness. The three of us shall draw lots. The shortest straw will be my dinner. The lucky one may pass through the door."

"And what if it's you who draws the short straw?" Brian asked.

"Then you both walk out," Owen said. "And I wait until Josephus sends me one of his smaller gifts."

Brian saw John look from Owen to the door, and he knew the man contemplated a run for it.

Owen noticed as well.

"I can assure you," Owen said softly, "I am far, *far* stronger than I look. You would not be the first meal I've had to shoot on the run."

John glared at the man, but he took a step back.

"Excellent," Owen said, keeping the pistol aimed at John. "Now, we simply need something so we can draw our lots."

Owen's eyes roamed away from John for a brief moment, and John charged him.

Before Brian could call out for him to stop, the older man had thrown himself at Owen. The two men and the chair went over, the pistol barking twice in the room.

Brian ran around the side of the table and came to a sharp stop.

John was dead.

He had an exit wound the size of a fist in the center of his back. The man lay sprawled across Owen, who was crushed beneath John's weight and pressed against the chair.

Owen was dying. The skeletal man gasped for each breath, and Brian knew Owen's weakened body could not push John's dead weight off. Brian felt neither pity nor compassion for the cannibal.

It took Owen a long time to die, and then Brian realized he was alone in the Paupers' Crypt.

CHAPTER 24
AN UNPLEASANT DISCOVERY

Josephus felt the gunshots, and he smiled.

Owen had played his part, as Josephus had known the man would.

Time was no longer what it had once been for Josephus. He had lost his sense of it when he was imprisoned; death had not returned the perspective to him. Hours could pass, and he would surface amongst the living only to discover it had been months or years. At other times, he could sit for a decade in the darkness and learn that less than a week had passed in the light of the sun.

There was something dark and twisted about the Crypt. It had been there before Josephus' arrival, and it would remain after his departure, if such a thing were ever to occur.

All of this passed through his mind as Josephus made his way easily through the warren of passages and rooms which existed in the Crypt's special world. He knew his way to Owen's room; he had fashioned it himself before he had put the prisoner in there.

Owen, a portly man, now, nothing more than skin and bones and appetite.

The image of the gaunt cannibal made Josephus smile as he opened the door to Owen's room with some excitement. He was certain the man would be carving his dinner into acceptable portions.

Yet Owen was not in his chair. The chair was not even at the table.

Confused, Josephus made his way towards the far door only to come upon a strange scene. Owen and the other man, dead.

Brian had slipped away.

Rage flooded through Josephus, and he turned upon the bodies. Both of the spirits were hiding. Movement caught his attention and Josephus looked under the table.

Owen's ghost hid beneath it.

Josephus smiled, reached out and grabbed Owen quickly before he could slip away. The man's spirit babbled incoherently and tried to wriggle away, pulling and sliding between Josephus' fingers. But Josephus merely smiled, brought Owen closer. He was far too strong, too powerful for someone as pitiful as Owen to resist. With a pleased chuckle, Josephus slowly squeezed Owen's soul until the light in it faded.

Josephus grinned, for Owen's screams of terror and pain were delightfully refreshing.

CHAPTER 25
IN THE DARKNESS

Brian closed the door behind him and stood alone in the darkness. He had nothing with him. He had forgotten the light.

Part of him wanted to turn around and see if he could find the door handle, but that wasn't an option. He was afraid to return to Owen's room. There was always the chance that the spirits of both John and Owen could come back.

Back was the wrong way to go; he needed to get out of the crypt, immediately.

Brian stood in the darkness of the newest room. He tried to close his eyes but felt dizzy when he did. Frowning, Brian reached out, turned slightly to the right and found a wall. It was cold and felt like stone. Drops, of what he hoped were water, slipped around his fingertips, and he began to walk.

He never lost contact with the wall, and he took small steps. The floor felt smooth beneath his shoes, and he had no desire to fall in a hole or to trip over something in the darkness.

In his ears, he heard his heart thump. His breaths came in long and slow. He continued to move along the wall. He smelled water and earth. Nothing more. His footsteps were muffled, as though there was something which deadened the sound in the room.

Images flashed through his mind. Owen and John. Malachi and Mitchell. The ghosts in the cemetery. Jenny smiling at him.

The last image made him happy, and he tried to focus on her as he continued on.

He tried to check his phone, to see what the time was, but when he took it out of his pocket and tried to see it, nothing happened. After several attempts, he realized the battery was dead, and he dropped it back into his pocket

Brian decided he would count his footsteps, to keep himself occupied. He stopped at one thousand. The counting was helping.

His stomach growled. An image of Owen flashed before him, and his desire to eat vanished.

"Brian."

He stopped and looked around. Someone had called his name. A man.

Brian opened his mouth to reply and then stopped.

What if there wasn't anyone? Brian wondered.

What if someone is waiting for me to speak? Brian thought. *What if someone is hunting me and merely wondering where I am in the room?*

Brian continued to move forward.

"We know you're in here, Brian," a voice said.

He couldn't tell if it was a man or a woman.

Something cold brushed against his arm.

"Are you close to us?" a second voice asked.

"Closer than he wants to admit," said the first.

He heard someone chuckle and say, "We'll find him, soon."

With the next words spoken, Brian could hear no difference. It was as if the two voices had become one.

"True. We have enough time, and he's lost."

"Alice down the rabbit hole."

"Eat me, drink me."

"Shh. You'll remind him of Owen."

Horrible images flashed through Brian's mind. He had a sudden, irrational fear that John was still alive, and that Owen had been only pretending. Brian vividly imagined how John would have been butchered efficiently. Owen would be sitting in his chair. Brian pictured blood spilling out of the corners of Owen's mouth as the man took small, delicate pieces of John's liver and chewed them methodically.

Owen's dead, Brian told himself sharply.

"Is he, though? You're stronger than we thought, Brian."

"Stronger than any of us thought. To be honest, we thought you wouldn't have made it this far."

"Of course, Mitchell did help, which was rather unsporting of him."

"It does make the game rather more interesting, though, does it not, Brian?"

Brian didn't respond. He continued forward, each step cautious, his hand always on the wall.

"Will you stay down here with us, Brian?"

And Brian saw himself trapped, forever, never dying as he wandered in darkness. He could see himself, eyes blind, beard long, and clothes turned to rags. Two dark shapes near him, always questioning and wondering what to do with him.

Brian felt panic well up within him and nest in his throat almost threatening to erupt in an uncontrollable scream. He fought it back viciously, forcing the unwanted and base desire to flee, back into the darker recesses of his heart.

"Oh, he is strong. Far stronger than we knew. Do you think he'll escape Josephus?"

"No. Oh no. I think dear Brian is in for something far worse than he can imagine."

"Tell us, Brian, do you think you can defeat Josephus?"

A dark form suddenly filled his mind. Beautiful blue eyes peered out from the shape's depths and sought to punch through Brian's thoughts. Hatred poured out of those eyes.

"Yes, you see a glimpse of Josephus. You see your death."

"Come, Brian, come. You have days of walking left. Let us see what else we can pick from your mind."

A cold, needle of thought punched into his memories and spiders swarmed out.

Brian nearly staggered under the weight of the recollection.

His grandfather's garage. On a spring day, looking for old comic books in the rafters. Seeking boxes of his father's Batman and Superman stories.

Then the spiders.

Spiderlings. Recently hatched and ravenous.

Brian had never seen the web, nor had he spotted the hundreds of small shapes clinging to the rafters. He had crawled shirtless through them towards an old Army footlocker stored in the back. Brian was brave, as much as a ten-year-old could be. He was fearless, focused on the comics. He wanted to read about Lex Luthor and the Joker, Robin and Jimmy Olsen.

And he hadn't noticed the spiders.

Their webs had wrapped around his flesh, fine strands of silk he had barely felt. He could feel them crawling on his back and shoulders. The faint caresses of hundreds of legs. He had thought it was the heat of the attic, the disagreeable act of sweating.

Then the biting had begun, and he had stopped, surprised.

The pain was nearly instantaneous.

Dozens of bites, scores of them. Hundreds of them.

He had yelled in both shock and horror. He had beaten his shoulders and back and then his neck until his hands ached. Finally, satisfied they had been killed, Brian had fled back the way he had come, only to move into another nest of recently hatched spiders.

Fear had overtaken him, driven him to the edge of awareness and he had fallen out of the garage's trap door. Four feet down and onto the roof of the 1967 Impala his father had been restoring.

The spiderlings had continued to bite him.

Brian shuddered, came to a brief stop until the memory and the phantom pain of the old bites passed. With a deep breath, he pushed on.

"Let us see what else is there," the first voice said.

The cold pierced his mind again, and Brian forced himself to walk on.

CHAPTER 26

RESEARCHING, 4:00 PM, MAY 2ND, 2016

Jenny's head hurt.

She sat on the floor in Leo's old building. Piles of books surrounded her. She had a notebook and a pen. There were only a few sentences jotted down on the open page. Barely a hundred words after hours of research.

Jenny closed her eyes, leaned against the wall and took a long, deep breath.

Shane had left an hour earlier. He had gone back to his house to see if Carl had come up with anything.

With a sigh, Jenny opened her eyes and looked at the last book she had pulled from the shelves. It was short and thin, bound in a beautiful marbled cover. The title was written in gold letters down the spine: *The World Behind Ours*, by Anonymous.

Leo's information on the book had been scant. It had held only the title, the unknown author, the date of publication, which was listed as "1932 (?)", and the single word 'Behind.' The word had been underlined several times.

Jenny picked it up, opened the book and began to read,

> *"It should come as no surprise to us, when we pause to actually consider the idea, that there is actually more to this world than we can see. The supernatural and the paranormal are often scoffed at by traditional scientists and those who cling to the narrow boundaries of the scientific principle. There is a large part of the scientific and rational community who believe if it cannot be seen, it cannot exist.*

"This faulty logic is what kept the world in darkness and believing it was flat, as well.

"We believe in a Heaven and a Hell, and the Catholics believe in a Purgatory. Could there not be another world, perhaps even multiple worlds, which exist in the shadows of ours?

"We cannot deny the existence of ghosts, although the naysayers howl out their disagreement. They declare the idea of spirits is both primitive and barbaric. Yet the evidence, although it cannot be repeated upon demand, is there. Recordings of hauntings have been made for as long as there have been people to jot them down, and it continues.

"This small book is not a defense of the supernatural. You, the reader, must accept the supernatural as an undeniable truth or else you shall gain no benefit from this work. My goal here is to examine the evidence of a world behind ours, one which is in its shadow. This shadow world is ever-present, and sometimes we interact with it, although we are usually unaware.

"Occasionally, however, stories arise of the shadow world breaking into ours. They are often fearful tales of being trapped, unable to return to our own place and our own time. There are many tales of such occurrences, perhaps the most famous one being that of Rip Van Winkle. We must ask ourselves was this really a story, or perhaps some bit of history Washington Irving was privy to.

"A telltale sign of this hidden world slipping into ours is the unexplained arrival of large swaths of fog…"

Jenny stopped, reread the line several times and felt her heartbeat quicken.

Fog, she thought. *The fog.*
With shaking hands, Jenny read on.

CHAPTER 27

SHANE GETS INFORMATION, 4:00 PM, MAY 2ND, 2016

"It is not good news, I am afraid, my young friend," Carl said.

Shane poured himself a whiskey and looked at Carl. "Tell me."

"This fog," Carl said, "it is a gate, a door, if you will, from one part of the world into another. Much like the upper levels of your home, yes?"

"Yes," Shane said. He brought the tumbler and the whiskey to the table and sat down.

"This house," Carl said, drifting over to the table and standing across from Shane, "the barrier between the shadow world and this one is thin here. Partly, it is because of the number of deaths. And partly, because of the dark ones being imprisoned here. So many little factors which, when combined, create what we have here. The fog, though, it is disturbing."

"Why?" Shane asked.

"Because if what your friend's wife says is true, then it means you are dealing with a spirit who has the power to open a passage between the shadow world and yours, at will. This spirit has the strength to pull people into the shadow world, and to actually deny entrance back into the real, physical world." Carl shook his head. "This is an incredible power. It is not to be approached lightly."

"Can we do something to help my friend?" Shane asked.

"Yes, but you must approach it with care," Carl said. "First, you must find a way into the shadow world. Here, you are well familiar with Berkley Street. You know what doors to open, what paths to take. In this cemetery, well, you will need to discover it. You must find the door, and you must go in armed."

"With what?" Shane said, taking a drink. "What can I fight the dead with, other than iron?"

"I do not know," Carl said, "but you must find out before you go. Your life, and your friend's life, both will depend on it."

CHAPTER 28

MOVING ON

It took Brian a moment to realize his hand had left the stone of the wall and felt wood.

He stopped, his throat convulsing. He forced all other thoughts from his mind, including the voices. They had plumbed the depths of his memories, sought out horrors from his childhood. Base fears had been dragged up and presented with all of their original terror.

Brian brought his left hand to join his right, and together they explored the wood. It was smooth and pleasant to the touch. He found cold, metal hinges. A knob which felt like porcelain. He licked his lips nervously, turned the doorknob and pulled.

An involuntary cry was torn from his throat as light burst into the darkness.

Yet he was too afraid to let go of the porcelain. He held onto it dearly, as though his life depended on it.

Brian covered his eyes with his left hand and fought the urge to race into the brightness. Although darkness and terror lay behind him, he was unsure as to what waited for him beyond the doorway.

His heart beat mutinously against his chest, and he waited, willed it to slow down, and forced his body to comply. Whether it was seconds, minutes, or hours until he had control over himself, Brian didn't know. When he did, he opened his eyes.

A small room stood before him. There was a door on the right wall. A door on the left. The walls were painted a bright white, and the floor was of wood. The ceiling looked to be made of stamped tin panels. The room was lit by a small metal lamp, cast to look like a pair of winged cherubs, standing on a short and narrow side table. Beside the table was a pile of neatly folded blankets. To the right of those was a large glass bottle of what looked like water and a stack of canned goods.

Brian's stomach immediately growled at the sight of the food and drink.

He took a deep breath and looked around the room before he entered. He couldn't see anyone else, but he could smell them. The distinct human scent of sweat and despair.

Brian paused, closed the door behind him, and walked stiffly to the blankets and the food. He bent down, his hands shaking as he lifted the bottle up and uncorked it. For a moment, he thought about the possibility of the water being poisoned, and then he didn't care.

He was too thirsty. He took several long drinks, his body screaming for the water. But he didn't allow himself to drink it all. Who knew why the water was there, or when Brian might be able to have more. Reluctantly, he corked the bottle and returned it to its place.

Next, he looked at the canned food; green beans, corn, spam and baked beans. He lifted the last, saw an old fashioned can opener next to the blankets and nearly wept with joy. In moments, he had the baked beans open, and he ate them as slowly as he could. He was ravenous, as though he hadn't eaten in days instead of mere hours.

And what if it has been days? Brian wondered after he had finished. He put the can down and stared at it. He thought about the stories John had told him, the tales of people who claimed to have been trapped for days in the cemetery.

He tried not to think about it and looked, instead, at the blankets.

Brian was tired. Exhausted. He needed to sleep, and while no place would be safe, he could at least be warm. Silently, he took off the first blanket, an old comforter whose pattern had long faded away. While the fabric was threadbare and aged, it felt good and safe. Brian wrapped up in it and laid down, resting his head on the other blankets. He closed his eyes and opened them again immediately, afraid of the darkness.

You have to rest, he told himself.

Once more, he closed his eyes and fought to keep them shut. He brought up a memory of Jenny. She sat in her chair, crocheting a scarf. It was in the old house, the one in Manchester. The split-level on Hanover Street. Before they had moved out to Mont Vernon for his health.

Brian smiled at the memory, and he let himself relax.

"Who are you?" the voice was soft and caused Brian's eyes to snap open.

A man, older than Brian, stood near the door on the left. His clothes had seen better days and his hair was long and gray. The man's beard was the same, his eyes were a deep hazel and his skin was exceptionally pale. In one hand, he held a plastic trash bag with something in it. His other hand held a wicked-looking knife. The man was thin, but not emaciated.

"May I sit up?" Brian asked.

The man nodded.

Carefully and slowly, Brian slipped his hands-free of the blanket so the man could see them. Then Brian sat up.

"You ate my beans," the man said.

"Yes," Brian said. "I was hungry. I'm sorry."

The man shrugged and sat down across from Brian. "Saves me the trouble of eating them. I hate 'em. Found three cases of them a while ago. You get tired of some things real quick. Even when you're hungry."

He put the knife down beside him and looked at Brian. "When were you born?"

"August first, 1973," Brian answered.

The man grunted, shook his head and said. "Hell. Been a lot longer than I thought."

"When were you born?" Brian asked.

"April second, 1950," the man answered. He extended his hand. "Jacob. Jacob Wurbach."

Brian shook it and introduced himself.

"Pleasure, Brian," Jacob said. He opened the plastic bag. He took out a battered plastic jug of water, a Matchbox car of a corvette, and a pair of old jeans. "My daily scavenging."

"How long have you been here?" Brian asked, unable to keep fear out of his voice.

Jacob looked at him for a moment before he answered. "Well, let me ask you this. How old are you, Brian?"

"Forty-two," Brian said.

"So, if I can still do math, it means the year is 2015 or there about?"

"Off by just a year," Brian said. "I'll be forty-three soon."

"Looks like I've been here for almost forty-four years then, although I know I don't look it," Jacob said. He squinted and looked at Brian. "You alright? You just got real pale."

Brian nodded. "Trying to wrap my head around this."

Jacob looked at him confusedly for a moment, and then he nodded, as though he just pieced together what Brian meant. "Fair enough. Now, in case you haven't figured it out, time is a little different here."

"Yeah," Brian said softly. "I met someone named Owen earlier."

Jacob snorted. "Surprised he's still alive. Miserable man."

"He's dead now," Brian said.

Jacob raised an eyebrow, and then he nodded. "Serves him right. Tried to shoot me once when I passed through. Damned cannibal. He was Josephus' pet."

"You know Josephus?" Brian asked.

"Let's say I know *of* him," Jacob replied. "Been avoiding him since I've been here."

"How come you're not starving?" Brian said. "How are you getting food?"

Jacob grinned. "I found the marsh."

"What?" Brian asked, shaking his head, confused.

"See," Jacob said, pulling on his beard thoughtfully, "I guess you got trapped by the fog."

Brian nodded.

"Well," Jacob said, "Josephus, he's rotten to the core and he pulls the fog out of the marsh. He does it to trap the living in the cemetery, and then he funnels them into this twisted world of his. So the fog is always there, some part of it anyway."

"The fog?" Brian asked.

Jacob nodded. "It's a way into here, wherever *here* is. I go out into the fog, rummage through the marsh. Just can't get out of it."

"Why?" Brian asked. "If it's just fog, why can't you get out? Why can't we?"

"The fog's a barrier," Jacob said after a moment. "Whether Josephus did it on his own, or if it was always as it is, I don't know. You can go in

80

and wander around all you want, but there's only two ways back into the crypt, once you're in the fog. One's a door I use, and the other's a little stream. It's too narrow and shallow for me to get into, but from what I've heard from some of the dead, it cuts into a small cave in the crypt."

"Don't you get lost out there?" Brian asked, feeling confused. "Haven't you been trapped out there?

"No," Jacob said. "I spent a couple of years in Vietnam, fighting the commies. This fog, it ain't nothing to me. Now I've tried like hell to get out of this place, but the fog hasn't ever let me. I may not be able to leave, but I can always find my way back here."

"And this is how you've been living?" Brian said.

Jacob nodded. "First couple of years, or however the hell long it's been, were a little rough. Lived a lot on frogs and roots and stuff I'd rather not think about. Then I started to find things. Cans of food here and there. Every once in a while some soda pop, or if I was really lucky, a beer or some liquor. Then clothes and things. The marsh bordered on the town dump, and I guess it's still spreading. I'm a regular Robinson Crusoe."

Brian laughed suddenly and shook his head.

Jacob looked at him warily. "What?"

"Guess that makes me your Friday," Brian said, grinning.

Jacob snorted with laughter, nodded his head and passed the jug of water over to Brian. "Take a drink, Friday. Let's celebrate."

CHAPTER 29

MAKING PREPARATIONS, 7:00 PM, MAY 2ND, 2016

"Thanks," Jenny said, accepting the water from Shane.

"No problem," he said, taking a seat across from her on the floor. He looked around at all of the books and asked, "So, any luck?"

"Yeah," she said, nodding and patting the book on her lap. "This book here, it talks about another world. One that's sort of behind ours."

"Carl said the same to me," Shane said. "He told me we would need to find a way in. And that we'd better arm ourselves."

"The book doesn't say that," Jenny said, frowning. "Although, I don't think the writer was thinking about some pain-in-the-ass ghost who thought it would be fun to drag my husband into his little world."

"True," Shane said. "Very true."

"The author does say, though," Jenny added, pausing to take a drink, "how the fog is a pretty standard way in and out of this shadow world. From what he said, if we find the right fog, we'll get in."

"So," Shane said, "We also need a weapon. Well, probably weapons. Carl said whoever is strong enough to shut down a whole cemetery is probably a little tough to handle."

"The only thing I know of is iron," Jenny said. She held up her hand to show Shane her iron ring.

He nodded. "Brian taught me about iron. I think we might need something a little more aggressive, though."

Jenny frowned and thought for a moment. "I know we used a shotgun loaded with rock salt once. That was pretty damned aggressive. We also bound ghosts before."

"No," Shane said, "I don't think a binding would work out that well. Not if we're in the guy's own house. The shotgun sounds good, though.

Do you have one?"

"There might be one here," she said after a moment. "We can check upstairs, in Leo's apartment."

"Okay," Shane said. "Sounds good. Think there are still shells for it?"

"I hope so," Jenny said.

"Well," Shane said, "if not, it's not a big deal. I'll go down and pick some up. I think we'll need to focus on finding a way in, though."

Jenny sighed and rubbed her temple. "How the hell are we going to do that? I don't suppose your friend, Carl, would be able to help?"

"No," Shane said, shaking his head. "He's bound to the house."

"Let me get in touch with some friends," Shane said. "They might be able to help."

"Okay," Jenny said. She looked around at the books and suddenly felt overwhelmed. "What now?"

"Now," Shane said, "I'll send a text to my friend, and we'll go check to see if that shotgun is still around."

"Sounds good" Jenny said tiredly. "I just want my Brian back."

"Understood," Shane said. He stood up and offered his hand.

Jenny smiled, took it, and got to her feet.

CHAPTER 30
SEEKING THE PREY

Josephus sat in Owen's room and looked at the remains of Owen's spirit. It never ceased to amaze him, the amount of agony a spirit could endure. A grayish white strip, all which remained of Owen's spirit, was spread on the floor.

Eventually, it would reform, and Owen's ghost would join the hundreds of others in the crypt.

Eventually.

Josephus smiled. The cannibal's pain had been delectable and quite made up for the escape of Brian.

Josephus looked around the room, searching. Tucked into a dark corner, barely visible, was what he sought.

The spirit of the other who had been with Brian.

"Come out," Josephus commanded.

The spirit didn't move.

Josephus frowned, reached out and grasped the ghost. The man snarled in pain as he was pulled into the open.

"You're willful," Josephus said, chuckling. The man twisted and pulled, trying to get free of Josephus. "No, no. None of that."

The man howled as Josephus squeezed for a moment.

When Josephus relaxed his grip, the man didn't struggle, merely glared at him.

"Excellent," Josephus said. "You learn quickly."

The man didn't reply.

Josephus shrugged. "You will seek out Brian, the one you were traveling with. When you find him, bring him to me."

"Do it yourself," the man snapped.

Josephus squeezed until the man screamed. He tightened his grip a little more. After a moment, he relaxed his hold and smiled. "I have things such as you to do the task for me. Do it well, and I will probably forget you even exist. Fail to find him, and each day, for a decade, I will make the cannibal's passing seem like a blessing in comparison to what you will suffer."

The man glanced around the room, at the shimmering remnants of Owen's ghostly body, and nodded.

"I'll find him," the man said.

"Excellent," Josephus said, letting go. "Do not rush. We have an abundance of time. Merely find him, and tell me where he is."

"Where will you be?" the man asked.

"In the crypt, by the door," Josephus replied. "And mark your passage. It is easy to get lost here."

Without waiting to see what the man would do, Josephus turned and left the room.

CHAPTER 31
A NEW FRIEND

Brian liked Jacob.

The man was funny and odd. But Brian figured solitary confinement for decades would make anyone quirky. Often, as they sat in Jacob's small room, the man would speak to himself. A low whisper. He would ask himself about the Boston Red Sox, who the president was and what the man was up to in office, and if a certain woman named Mary Anne was still single. He wondered what it would be like to eat a steak. He was curious about apple trees.

The first few times Jacob had spoken in a low voice Brian had answered him, and Jacob had looked up, surprised. Afterward, Brian had stopped. He only replied if Jacob spoke to him directly.

Which he did often enough.

"Brian," Jacob said.

Brian looked up and smiled tiredly. "Yes?"

"What's life like out there?" Jacob asked.

Brian stretched a little. "Well, it's different. I don't know much about the early seventies, I was a little too young, but I guess the best question is what do you want to know about specifically?"

Jacob thought for a moment before he answered, "Cars. I've seen a few pictures in newspapers and magazines I find. Not too many, though. The marsh water gets to them pretty quickly."

"Cars," Brian said, nodding. "Alright, let me tell you a little about cars."

He leaned back against the wall, took a sip from the jug of water, and told Jacob everything he knew about cars. He spoke for what was probably an hour, maybe even two. Jacob's eyes had grown wide at the size of the engines, and he had shaken his head at the speeds.

By the time Brian finished his throat was sore and he knew he hadn't covered a tenth of what there was to say. But Jacob was happy.

"A four hundred and forty-two-inch cubic engine," Jacob said, shaking his head. "And over a hundred and twenty miles an hour?"

Brian nodded.

"Police have those, too?" Jacob asked.

"They have what are called interceptors," Brian said. "I don't know much about those, other than they'll keep up with the best in a chase."

Jacob grinned, then he shook his head and sighed. "I miss driving. Was one of my favorite things to do. I'd take my old pickup, a fifty-seven Ford, and just drive for a while. Helped me to forget certain things."

Jacob pulled at his beard for a moment, muttered something about a fishing hole, and then he smiled. "So, you're married?"

"Yes," Brian said, looking down at his wedding ring.

"Tell me about her," Jacob said, closing his eyes.

Brian chuckled and began to talk about Jenny.

CHAPTER 32

TRYING TO SLEEP, 2:10 AM, MAY 3RD, 2016

Jenny hadn't gone home.

There was no point. Brian wasn't there, and she would have been tempted to go to the cemetery herself to see what she could do.

She lay on her back in Leo's small bed and stared up at the ceiling. The room still contained his favorite books as well as the battered old chair. It was almost completely dark, except for the bathroom light Jenny had turned on.

She closed her eyes and tried to breathe slowly. She doubted meditation would work, but it was worth a shot. As she tried to relax, she thought of the shotgun and the box of shells loaded with rock salt.

Shane had even mentioned iron knuckle-dusters, Jenny remembered. Then with a sigh, she thought, *And he still hasn't heard from his friends.*

The two of them would have to go into the cemetery alone. They had to find fog, and part of her wondered how hard it would be to spot fog, but she realized it probably wasn't going to be easy at all.

I just want him home, she thought, opening her eyes.

"I just want him home," she whispered into the darkness.

"What's going on?" someone asked.

Jenny screamed.

She sat up and looked around.

A faint, almost glowing shape stood off to the left. The darkness was thicker there, a bookcase blocking the light from the bathroom.

"What's wrong?" the voice asked again, and Jenny realized the voice was a woman's. Familiar even.

Jenny leaned forward slightly. Then, in a whisper, she asked, "Sylvia?"

The ghost of Sylvia Purvis stepped forward. Her hair hung down, and she wore a sweater and a multi-colored, floor-length skirt. And she smiled.

"How are you, Jenny?"

Jenny opened her mouth to answer, closed it and shook her head. "Sylvia? Oh my God, Sylvia! I've missed you so much!"

Her friend smiled, the warm, beautiful smile Jenny remembered so well.

"I've missed you, too, Jenny," Sylvia said. "Can you tell me what's wrong?"

"Brian," Jenny said, and before she could say anymore, she burst into tears.

For several long minutes, she cried, until finally the tears stopped and, sniffling, she was able to speak again.

Sylvia looked at her with concern.

"It's Brian," Jenny said, and she explained to Sylvia what had happened. When she had finished, there was a frown on Sylvia's face.

"This doesn't sound good, Jenny," Sylvia said after a moment.

Jenny nodded. "Shane said he was going to try and find someone, he hadn't heard from anyone before he left."

"I know someone who'll help you," Sylvia said.

"Who?" Jenny asked.

Sylvia smiled. "Leo."

"I thought of Leo, but I don't know how to reach him. You can get in touch with him?" Jenny said.

Sylvia raised an eyebrow and Jenny let out a laugh.

"Of course, you can," she said, shaking her head.

"I'll go and speak with him," Sylvia said. "We'll both return tomorrow, although I'm not sure exactly when. Time is, well, it's different for us."

"Okay," Jenny said. She hesitated and then she added, "It's really good to see you again, Sylvia."

"I feel the same," Sylvia said, smiling.

Sylvia vanished, leaving Jenny alone in Leo's room. She laid down again, closed her eyes, and felt exhaustion wash over her. Sleep pulled at her, and Jenny smiled. Leo would help her find Brian, and with the knowledge of the man's help, Jenny let herself rest.

CHAPTER 33
JOSEPHUS WAHLEN, SEPTEMBER 20TH, 1842

Josephus was in agony as he rolled across the grass, the morning dew soaking into his clothes. Sunlight filtered in through the flour sack they had tied around his head, and his wrists and ankles ached. The thick hemp cord which bound his limbs together cut into his flesh cruelly, and he wondered, dimly, when they had captured him.

He could remember drinking at the tavern. Sitting in a secluded corner while a plump serving girl kept his mug full. He vaguely recalled a piece of tough meat, and potatoes boiled to mush. The fire in the hearth had been terribly warm.

Joseph screamed as someone kicked him in the stomach.

Voices murmured, yet he couldn't understand them. Not a word. The blood pulsing in his head and muffling the world.

Hands gripped his arms harshly, and he was jerked up to his feet. Whoever it was didn't try to make him stand, but instead, they dragged him along. He tried to lift his head up, and he managed to ask, "Who?"

The reply was a vicious blow which shattered a tooth and mashed his lips. Blood exploded into his mouth, and he gagged.

A metal hinge creaked loudly and a dank, musty smell rolled over him. He could smell decay and rot, and what little light drifted in through the sack on his head faded to darkness.

A moment later, he was dropped roughly to the ground. He could smell dirt as he rolled onto his side, coughing. He fought hard to keep his stomach calm, but he failed. With a terrible retch, he vomited into the confines of the sack, the hot bile coating his face.

Someone swore loudly, and Josephus received another kick to the stomach, which made him throw up again.

He gasped and spat and curled into a ball.

As he lay on his side and tried to catch his breath, he heard someone squat down beside him. The ties on the sack were loosened, and it was pulled off his head. Josephus kept his eyes closed tightly.

"God, you're a mess, Josephus Wahlen," a voice said.

Josephus cracked an eye open and looked into the face of Daniel Norton. The old man's expression was grim, his brown eyes empty of any pity.

"Daniel," Josephus said, his voice rough and pained.

"You've been found out, sir," Daniel said. "And we know of the terrible crimes you've committed."

Josephus shook his head in denial.

"I've been in your house, Josephus," Daniel said coldly.

"Then you know there is nothing," Josephus responded.

"I found the false wall in your root cellar," Daniel said. His words were spoken harshly and with a note of finality.

A chill settled over Josephus as he tried to think of something to say.

If Daniel found the false wall, then he entered the room. And Josephus would find out what Hell looked like soon enough.

Daniel seemed to know the course of Josephus' thoughts. "Oh no," Daniel said softly, "you'll not be going to the Devil just yet, foul man."

"Imprisoned?" Josephus asked, laughing with unrepentant joy.

"In a manner of speaking," Daniel said. "Do you not recognize where you are?"

In truth, Josephus couldn't see much of anything, so he shook his head.

"You should, preacher," Daniel snarled, and he slapped Josephus viciously across the face. "You should. You stood here, in this crypt and spoke to Patience Dean's mother about the mercy and love of God. You offered her false sympathy, all the while it had been you who had killed her little girl. Butchered the child. You foul, wretched beast."

Josephus shook his head, trying to clear his thoughts.

The Dean girl had been buried in the Paupers' Crypt. The family, too poor for anything else.

The crypt.

"Ah," Daniel whispered. "You know now, don't you? What better

91

place for an evil man, than a place of evil? Didn't the Abenaki torture your grandfather in this cave? Didn't your father find him, flayed alive? Did he not beg for death? Yes, we all know the horrific torments carried out here. The rumors of the unquiet dead."

Josephus stiffened as fear spiked through him, and he twisted around.

Several men stood around him, and he could see the walls of the crypt beyond them. Further back, he caught sight of the open door which led to the rest of Wood's Cemetery. He shifted his body and saw another man, who he couldn't recognize. The man was standing by the inner crypt door, where those who had died of the pox had been buried.

"Why am I here?" Josephus demanded, trying to keep the fear out of his voice.

Daniel gave him a grim smile. "You are to be imprisoned. Here, among the dead."

Josephus licked his swollen lips and asked, "For how long?"

"What do you mean?" Daniel asked.

"How long is my sentence?" Josephus said, his voice shaking. "How long must I remain in the crypt before I am brought to trial and sent to prison?"

"This *is* your prison," Daniel said in a gentle voice. "Your sentence is death. By starvation. We will waste neither time nor food upon you. Nor will we afford you the opportunity of a trial. Hanging is too good for you, Josephus Wahlen. No. You will know fear. You will know hunger. And you will die in darkness, as did the girl you murdered."

Silence filled the crypt until Josephus broke it with a single word.

"No," he whispered.

"Yes," Daniel said, standing up. He nodded to the man by the door to the pox chamber, and Josephus heard it open. "Will you walk or be dragged in?"

Josephus went to say "walk," but instead, he screamed.

Before he could stop himself, Josephus began to beg and plead.

The reward, for his efforts, was a kick from Daniel, which broke several of his ribs.

Josephus gagged on the pain, stars exploding around his vision as Daniel grabbed hold of him by the neck of his coat. When Josephus found his voice, he screamed once more. But only once.

Before he could catch his breath for another, Daniel threw him into the pox room. A moment later, the man knelt down beside Josephus, and the hemp rope was quickly cut away.

Within a heartbeat, the door was slammed shut and locked after Daniel left.

Josephus caught his breath, listened, and he heard the sound of his prison cell being sealed.

Josephus was alone in the darkness, and with the dead.

His stomach rumbled.

CHAPTER 34
POLITE INQUIRIES ARE MADE, 7:00 AM, MAY 3RD, 2016

Jenny woke up and stretched, rolled over, and shrieked.

Leo's eyes widened, and he nearly vanished. For a moment, he was barely visible, merely a hint of a form in his old chair. Then he was solid once more.

He looked around the room and said, "What is it, Jennifer Roy?"

Jenny had to wait a moment for her heart to stop pounding. With a deep breath, she sat up, looked at Leo and said, "I was surprised to see you."

"Why?" Leo asked, genuinely confused. "Did Sylvia not tell you she was coming to find me?"

"She did," Jenny admitted.

"This is my house, is it not?" Leo asked, still searching for the reason why Jenny might be confused.

"It is," Jenny agreed.

"Therefore," Leo said, "would it not be logical for me to be here if Sylvia sought me out and this house is mine?"

"Never mind, Leo," Jenny said, sighing. She took the blankets and sheet off, swung her legs off the bed and was glad she had slept in her clothes. Dead or not, it might have proven to be too much for Leo to handle. She leaned forward, took her boots out from under the bed and put them on.

Leo waited politely until she had finished before he said, "Brian Roy is in trouble."

Jenny nodded.

"Sylvia," Leo continued, "told me about the situation in which he finds himself. He is bound within a cemetery. A crypt, to be specific?"

"Yes," Jenny said.

"There is a door, from this world to another, via a fog," Leo said. "And by means of this fog, the ghost is able to entrap and imprison."

"Evidently," Jenny said. Her patience was thin and Leo was always a challenge, alive or dead.

"Our first effort must be to locate this fog," Leo said after a moment. Jenny only nodded.

"From there, I will need to try and go into the crypt," Leo continued. "This way, I will be able to locate Brian. Whether alive or dead, I will be able to find him."

"Leo," Jenny said, holding up a hand.

"Yes, Jennifer Roy?" he asked.

"Please," she said, "I don't want to entertain the idea of Brian being dead."

He opened his mouth, then closed it and nodded instead.

Jenny took a deep breath, closed her eyes and gathered her thoughts. Exhaling slowly, she looked once more at Leo. "Now, Leo, do you know how long it will take to find him?"

"I do not," Leo answered.

"Why, Leo?" she asked, trying to remain patient.

"If this spirit is strong enough to cordon off a large area of the physical world, then there is no telling how much he has manipulated his own world," Leo said.

"What do you mean?" Jenny said. "I don't understand."

"Think of it as construction, Jennifer Roy," Leo said. "When this building was built, it required a large number of men and materials. If this spirit is strong enough to build a wall of fog, then there is no telling what he may have constructed within the crypt. Some spirits are able to create a single room in which to hide. I suspect there might be more, *many* more rooms."

"Jesus," Jenny muttered. "This keeps getting better and better."

"Jennifer Roy," Leo said.

"Yes, Leo?" she asked, looking at him.

"I fail to understand how this situation continues to become better," he said.

Jenny shook her head, laughed and stood up. "Don't worry about it, Leo. Don't worry about it. I need coffee."

He smiled, then, with a concerned expression he said, "Jennifer Roy, caffeine is a serious addiction."

Jenny went to reply, stopped herself and decided it was better to get her coffee instead. She wanted to get to Shane's as soon as possible.

CHAPTER 35
JOHN GOES HUNTING

John didn't want to hunt Brian.

Then again, he didn't want to be tormented for decades by this devil either.

And John was fairly certain Josephus Wahlen was about one step below the Devil. As nice as Brian had been, John wasn't going to suffer for him.

He had left the cannibal's chamber as quickly as he could. With some distance between himself and Josephus, John had made a decision, and he moved with purpose.

John could hear the other dead whisper around him, but he paid them no mind.

They chatted among themselves about the fear some people had of spiders. When he had left them, they were wondering whether it would be better to be eaten by one large spider, or several hundred little ones.

The next door, John found, had led to a hall. The hall led to a rectangular corridor full of windows, each one looking into yet another room.

Whereupon there were more doors.

Hallways. Rooms. Doors. Windows.

None of them held Brian.

Or any trace of him.

Finally, with his patience nearing its end, John came to a small room, roughly the size of a broom closet, and he sat down. He was angry.

He doubted Josephus would accept anything other than Brian's exact location.

John was certain he didn't want to see another vicious display of Josephus' anger.

"Do you think there's a chance?"

John looked around.

Brian had spoken. The man's voice had come from the other side of the wall.

"Always a chance," an unknown man replied. "We'll have to go out later after we sleep."

"Christ," Brian said.

"What?" the other asked.

"I just want to be out now," Brian answered.

The man chuckled. "I've wanted the same thing for a very long time."

There was a lull in the conversation and then Brian asked, "What about Josephus?"

"What about him?" the man replied.

"Will we meet him in the fog?" Brian said.

"Doubt it," the other said. "He stays in mostly, unless he wraps the fog around the cemetery. Don't think he'll do it soon, though. He usually doesn't."

"Alright," Brian said. "Guess I need to try and sleep."

"The both of us," the man said. "The both of us."

The conversation ended, and John stood up.

I may not be able to reach him, John thought. *But, at least I know what he'll be doing.*

Armed with the information, John left the room and made his way back towards Josephus Wahlen.

CHAPTER 36

125 BERKLEY STREET, 8:15 AM, MAY 3RD, 2016

"I am impressed," Leo said.

Jenny looked over at the ghost, still slightly disturbed at being able to see through him when the sun peered through the overhead clouds. She asked, "Why are you impressed, Leo?"

"The house in front of us," Leo said. "I can see the multiple levels which extend beyond its physical form. Whoever constructed them was exceptionally strong."

"Leo," Jenny said, "are you okay?"

"I am dead, Jennifer," Leo replied.

She shook her head. "I know. I mean, well, you look a little, ah, thinner. I can see through you."

Leo nodded. "I am not feeling quite as strong as I usually do. When I am weaker, I lack the ability to be as solid as you normally see me. Does this explain my 'thinness,' Jennifer?"

Jenny was about to answer when she was distracted by the front door being opened. Shane came out, zipping up his sweatshirt and closing the door behind him.

"Are you going to lock it?" Jenny asked.

Shane grinned at her. "No need. Anyone breaks in, the ghosts will take care of it."

Leo solidified slightly, and Shane paused in surprise.

"Good morning, Shane Ryan," Leo said cheerfully.

"Good morning, Leo," Shane said, shaking his head. "Glad you're here."

"Thank you," Leo said. "I am glad I am here as well."

Shane chuckled. "Alright. So, what's the plan then?"

"We go to Wood's Cemetery in Mont Vernon," Jenny said. "We find the marsh. We find the fog. We get my husband out."

"Sounds simple enough," Shane said. "Anything else?"

Jenny nodded. "Kill anything that gets in my way."

"I like it," Shane said. "We'll, I'm ready if you are."

"Damn straight," Jenny replied. She looked at Leo. "Anything you can think of, Leo?"

"In regards to our plan of action?" Leo asked.

"Yes," she said.

"All I can add," Leo said, "is we must be wary. If the fog is a true portal, then we must not underestimate the one who opened it. To do so, would be the death of both of you, and possibly the banishment of myself to the afterlife."

"Oh," Shane said. "Good. So long as there isn't any pressure."

Jenny gave both the dead man and the living one a hard smile. "No. No pressure at all."

She led the way to her car and tried to ignore the way Leo passed through the glass and steel to sit in the back seat. For a moment, her mind attempted to understand the physics of such a move, but then she shook the idea away.

She got into the car, waited until Shane was in, and then started the engine.

It was time to find Brian.

CHAPTER 37

THE ESCAPE BEGINS

Brian woke up with a start. For a moment, he lay panting on the floor, staring up at the plain, unadorned ceiling. When his heart returned to a normal rhythm, he sat up and saw Jacob.

The older man was braiding a rope out of strips of cloth. He paused, looked at Brian and asked gently, "Who's the King?"

Brian almost asked 'what', but he stopped himself.

He had been dreaming of the King of Middlebury. The nightmare of the Sanitarium. In the dream, he had been trapped in the tunnels beneath, a faceless man hunting him.

"Before this little journey into, well, whatever it is," Brian said, grimacing as he stretched. "I did a little bit of ghost hunting."

"Ghost hunting?" Jacob asked. "Now why in the hell would you do something like that?"

Brian shrugged. "Seemed like a good idea at the time."

Jacob shook his head, finished the last of the braid and tied it off. "You need to rethink your idea of a good time, Brian."

"I did," Brian replied. "I took the job as caretaker here and swore off anything else to do with ghosts."

"Guess they decided differently," Jacob said. "Here, catch."

He tossed an end of the rope to Brian, who caught it easily. Brian gave it a couple of tugs, found the braid to be strong and asked, "What's this for?"

"Going to tie us together," Jacob said. "This place gets a little hairy, and you don't know it the way I do."

Brian nodded.

"I'll tie one end around my waist, you tie the other around your waist, and we'll have about six feet of slack between," Jacob said. "We keep moving. We don't stop."

"Like the French Foreign Legion," Brian said.

"Yes," Jacob agreed. "March or die."

Brian stood up. He looked at Jacob and said, "We're going to make it out of here."

After a moment, Jacob said softly, "I've been trying for years. I'll give it another go, of course, but you need to understand, I haven't found the way out, yet. And I look each and every time I walk out the door."

"I know," Brian said, "but this time is different."

Jacob didn't answer. He stood up, tied one end of the rope around his waist and nodded for Brian to do the same.

Brian did so, making sure it was tight. "Do we need to bring anything?"

"No," Jacob said, shaking his head. "Funny thing about the fog, when you're done trying to escape, just turn around and the way back in, is there. Waiting for you."

The idea of it sent a chill down Brian's back. "Sounds absolutely terrible."

"It is," Jacob said, smiling tightly. "It sure is."

The older man looked around, nodded to himself, and without another word, turned to the door. He opened it quickly.

Beyond him, Brian saw a long, seemingly endless hallway made of dull glass walls and ceiling. The floor was made of packed dirt.

Jacob glanced at Brian and said, "Keep your eyes on me. Don't look left. Don't look right. There are things on the other side of the glass which aren't good to see."

Brian looked again and caught a glimpse of something fish-belly white. With a shock, he realized it was a face, the mouth was a vivid red, looking like a gaping wound. The eyes were black sockets, the nose gone. The flesh was flabby and jiggled obscenely as the creature turned its attention to the door.

"That's Bob," Jacob said softly. "He's the welcoming committee. He's the prettiest one. The others, well, they're even more disturbing."

Brian swallowed nervously, locked his eyes on Jacob and said, "Let's go."

Jacob nodded, turned away and began to walk down the hall.

Brian made sure to keep his eyes fixed firmly on the back of Jacob's skull, and did his best to ignore the shapes pressing themselves to the glass.

CHAPTER 38

IN THE CRYPT, 1842

He remembered the feast before he had been caught and imprisoned.

Josephus had eaten all of them. Every delectable bit of the young women he had slain. Sacrificed. He had devoured their souls, and he was stronger than anyone could imagine.

Yet the strength he had imbued did not permit him to escape the crypt.

It was a spiritual superiority, not physical.

So he remained trapped.

At first, he had gagged down the old and rotten flesh of Marcus Wetherbee, who had died a few weeks earlier of an unknown disease. His body had been placed in the pox crypt. Its rotting smell had gone from nauseating to delectable, the hungrier Josephus had become.

Water, too, had been a concern, but there was a small tunnel in the back of the pox crypt.

And it led to a small stream.

Josephus had heard the whisper of the water as it moved, and at first, he had believed it was only a hallucination. Yet, he had followed the tunnel, squeezed through narrow choke points where the whole weight of the earth seemed to press down upon him. Then he was through.

He could see nothing at all in the darkness, but he had crawled forward cautiously. His fingers had found the cold water, and he had drunk from the stream deeply.

Water was not all there was in the little cave he had found. There was so much more.

He had found slow moving fish, and plants which had drifted through. Even the occasional rat drew in.

Josephus had eaten everything he could catch and kill. Nothing was too foul; not when he was starving. As he ate and kept himself alive, Josephus planned his revenge.

Escape, he knew, was not an option open to him.

His vengeance would come soon. He would punish them for centuries.

Josephus lay upon his back, his left hand caressing the water while his right made swirls on the dirt floor of the cave. Although he could see nothing, he stared up. He recalled the eyes of the girls, how each had popped sensually in his mouth. He remembered the taste of them.

Josephus shuddered and was surprised as he felt a door open between the worlds.

The shadow behind reality stepped forward, and Josephus plunged in with his bounty of souls.

His body trembled once and then went still. His hands went limp. A small minnow, drawn by the sudden motion in the water, swam up to the fingers which broke the surface. It found the flesh, nipped at it, and then swam away.

It would return when the flesh fell away from the bone.

Josephus stood above his body, looked around the cave and saw it for the first time. He smiled, turned to the enslaved girls and said coldly, "It is time."

CHAPTER 39

WOOD'S CEMETERY, 9:15 AM, MAY 3RD, 2016

Jenny parked the car, turned off the engine and got out.

Leo was already standing beside the trunk and looking far thinner than before. Shane came out into the open air, a moment later.

"This place is bad," Leo said. He looked at Jenny. "It is very bad."

Jenny nodded. She knew it. Brian was trapped.

She popped the trunk with the key and went around to get the shotgun. She loaded it, checked the pump action on it, and slipped extra shells into her pockets. Jenny glanced over at Shane and saw him slip a pair of – what looked like – brass knuckles onto his right hand. They weren't brass, though, but iron.

"Iron," Jenny said, nodding her approval and wiggling her fingers at him, her own ring catching the sunlight.

"Yes indeed," Shane said, grinning and flexing his hand. "These worked out alright up in Rye."

"Leo," Jenny said.

"Yes, Jennifer Roy?" Leo asked.

"The fog's really pulled back. Do you know where the rest of it might be?" she said.

"In the marsh," he answered.

"Anywhere in particular in the marsh?" she asked, keeping a tight hold on her frustration.

Leo nodded. "In the far reaches of it you will find the entrance. While you travel to it I shall move ahead and enter the shadow world."

"Alright" Jenny said. "Shane and I will move to the back, to where the marsh is. The fog will be easy to see?"

"Yes," Leo said. "Once I am in the shadow world I will find Brian. When you are in the marsh, the fog will look like fog. It may not be large.

In fact, it may seem like a mere wisp. When you find it, wait for me there. When I have located Brian, I will meet with you and then be able to lead you both in and out of the shadow world."

"I don't like the idea of waiting," Jenny said, anxious. "Can't we just go in with you?"

Leo shook his head. "You cannot, Jennifer Roy. I must find him quickly. It will be difficult for us to escape this place. The one who controls it is strong. We must be careful."

"Nothing like the potential of being lost in another world," Shane said in a low voice.

"I know," Jenny said. "You don't have to come, Shane."

"No," Shane said. "I do. I like Brian, and I can't leave him trapped."

"Thank you," Jenny said. She shouldered the shotgun and looked at Leo. "We'll wait for you when we reach the fog. How will you know, though?"

"Know what?" Leo asked.

Jenny rolled her eyes, sighed and said, "When we get to the fog."

"Oh. Yes. Call out to me. I will hear you," Leo said.

"Even in the shadow world?" Jenny asked, skeptical.

Leo nodded. "If I am listening for someone, I will hear them. I will be listening for you, Jennifer Roy."

"Thank you, Leo," she said.

Leo smiled and vanished.

Jenny looked at Shane and asked, "Ready?"

The man nodded.

Silently, Jenny turned and headed to the left. She wondered if she would see Ruth when they reached the fog.

Or worse, if they would see Josephus.

Jenny focused on the task at hand and walked through the unmown grass. They followed the perimeter of the wrought iron fence and turned right when it did. Ahead of them, a tree line ran along a little piece of land and then dipped down. A small path, trampled down and littered with beer cans and other trash, led down and into tall reeds and cattails. The plants bent back with a slight wind and Jenny's nose wrinkled at the stale smell of the marsh.

The path they followed curled off to the right, still following the fence, but Jenny and Shane pushed on into the marsh. Within moments, her feet were wet and the smell grew worse as the mud beneath the still water was churned up. Trash floated by and birds called out from around them.

Her feet grew cold, her legs tired, but Jenny remained focused.

She needed to find a way in.

She would deal with any inconvenience.

CHAPTER 40

JOHN'S REPORT

John found Josephus in the cannibal's room. Josephus stood there, by the table, patiently stacking glasses one on top of the other. When John entered, Josephus looked up and gave him a smile which stopped John in his tracks.

"I hope," Josephus said, turning back to the dishes, "you have brought me news."

"I have," John replied.

"Out with it then," Josephus said. He picked up a knife, balanced it on top of the rim of the top most glass, and glanced again at John.

"I found Brian," John said.

His smile broadened. "Where?"

"I'm not sure," John said, and the smile vanished. "But I heard where he is planning to go."

Josephus frowned and turned away from his sculpture. "What do you mean?"

"He was speaking with another man," John said hurriedly. "They were talking about leaving the crypt for the marsh. Brian thinks he can escape through the fog."

"Another man?" Josephus said softly. "Another man."

"Yes," John said. He opened his mouth to say more, but the expression of anger which flashed across Joesphus' face silenced him.

"*Him!*" Josephus hissed. "He is still alive. After all this time. I thought he was lost forever in the fog. And they're heading there, to the fog?"

John could only nod.

"Come then," Josephus said, "we go to the fog as well. I've no time to toy with Brian. Not when the other is here still."

"Who's the other?" John asked, confused.

"Jacob Wurbach," he spat. "I'll eat his soul before the day is through."
John remained silent and followed the angry ghost out of the room.

CHAPTER 41

LOST AND FOUND

Brian didn't want to sleep ever again.

They had been walking for over an hour, at least, and they still hadn't left the hall of horrors. Even though he tried to keep his eyes averted, Brian occasionally looked to either side, and what he saw horrified him. The people beyond the glass were terrifying.

They ate one another, destroyed the flesh of those around them. He saw children eating adults, and adults eating children. He saw desecrations he had never imagined, and he felt certain he would suffer his final heart attack because of it.

He tried to close his eyes, and to walk blindly behind Jacob, but against the back of his eyelids, he saw the images. The pale white flesh, the bleeding wounds, the broken bones and black mouths sucking out the marrow.

He continued to stare at the small of Jacob's back, and he wondered how the man survived his travels.

"We're coming to the next door," Jacob said suddenly, breaking the silence.

"What's next?" Brian whispered hoarsely.

"A biting, punishing cold," Jacob replied. "Whatever you do, don't stop moving. Here we go."

Jacob stopped, and Brian heard him open a door.

A painful wind blasted out of the doorway, slamming into Brian and biting at all of his exposed skin.

Without another word, Jacob walked into the new room, and Brian followed. A dull light filled the air, and the room was huge, larger than anything Brian had seen so far. The ceiling was several stories high, and the walls were an easy one thousand feet from one another. Snow covered the floor, and the wood-paneled walls were covered with frost. Men and women, naked and frozen were scattered about, as though someone had paid a morbid tribute to Narnia's White Witch. The expressions on the dead were painful to look upon.

At the far right corner of the room, Brian caught sight of a small door, and he wondered how long it would take them to reach it. He could feel the cold sapping his strength. By the time he had taken twenty steps, his body had gone from horribly cold to painfully hot.

One of the first symptoms of hypothermia.

As soon as he recognized it, his mind spun out of control. Part of him wanted to strip off his clothes so he wouldn't be so terribly hot. The other part fought to keep them on.

Jacob stumbled, fell to a knee and then slowly got back to his feet. He shook his head and started to walk forward again.

Brian forced his legs to listen, to obey his commands. If he fell, he would die.

If Jacob couldn't free himself of the braided tether, he would die, too.

The door drew nearer.

Each step became a struggle. A battle to move onward. Brian no longer felt his ears or the tip of his nose. He felt as though his feet were encased in ice and as though his hands had been lopped off at the wrist.

Then, they were at the door, which opened of its own accord.

Leo, slightly more faded than usual, stood in it, looking at them with surprise and pleasure.

"Brian Roy!" Leo said excitedly. "I am pleased to have found you here."

Whether Leo was going to say more, Brian didn't know. Jacob pitched forward through the doorway and dragged Brian down with him.

CHAPTER 42

IN THE MARSH, 5:27 PM, MAY 3RD, 2016

"Jenny, there it is," Shane said, his voice thick with exhaustion. His finger trembled slightly as he pointed.

Jenny looked.

"Oh my God," she whispered. A wave of relief swept over her. Leo had never told them how far into the marsh the fog was, or how difficult it might be to reach it.

Fifteen feet away, barely visible behind the wreck of an old, 1930's pickup truck, was a bit of fog. It hung low to the water, moving lazily through and around the rusted body of the vehicle. The fog was thickest in the truck. The glass, Jenny noticed, was surprisingly intact. None of it had been broken.

"I'm going to call Leo," Jenny said.

Shane nodded and leaned against a scrub pine which grew awkwardly from a small tuft of solid land.

Jenny wet her lips and yelled out, "Leo!"

Nothing happened.

Jenny looked around. "Do you see him?"

Shane shook his head.

"Damn it," Jenny said, frowning. She waited, counted to thirty, and then yelled again, "Leo!"

Leo didn't show up.

She tightened her grip on the shotgun, turned around to see if maybe the dead man might be somewhere else, and then bit her tongue to keep herself from swearing.

Jenny took a deep breath, counted to sixty, and called out, "Leo!"

"What?"

Jenny jumped back, startled. Leo stood beside her.

She was so surprised that she could only point at the truck.

Leo looked and smiled. "Yes, it is the fog."

"What about you?" she managed to ask.

"What about me?" Leo asked politely, looking at her.

Jenny couldn't even answer.

Shane did, though.

"Leo," he said, "did you find Brian?"

"Oh, yes," Leo said happily.

After he didn't' say anything else, Jenny asked, "Leo, can you take us to him?"

"Well," Leo said, "we will have to go through the fog first."

"Yes," she said tightly. "I know."

"Oh, yes, very good," Leo said, nodding. "Very good. I will lead the way in. Follow me. The fog is both a barrier and a gateway into the shadow world, a hallway of sorts, if you will. When we reach the shadow world, I may have to leave you shortly so I might be able to get my sense of direction."

"Great," she said. "Fantastic. Do you want to open the truck door?"

"Yes," Leo said. With a gesture, the metal of the truck screamed as the entire door was ripped from its hinges and thrown into the marsh.

Jenny felt her eyes widen, and she looked over at Shane.

The man had straightened up, looked from Leo to the new hole in the truck and shook his head. "There's a new way to open a door."

Leo smiled. "Shall we?"

Jenny chambered a round into the shotgun, forgot about the cold and the pain of hours of walking through the marsh, and followed Leo into the truck. Shane was close behind her, and a moment later, she was in the thick fog where she had met Ruth.

"Jesus Christ," Shane said, "this is strange."

Jenny could only nod. Her stomach twisted slightly, as though it was being turned upside down.

Then the fog parted, and the three of them stood in a small room. The walls were painted bright white, the linoleum of the floor was pale blue, and the door across from them was bright red.

"I will return shortly," Leo said, and he vanished through a wall.

"Freaks me out when he does that," Shane murmured.

Jenny nodded her agreement. She kept her eyes on the wall and waited for Leo to return.

CHAPTER 43
WARMING UP

===

"Brian," Jacob said.

Brian opened his eyes and shivered.

"Here," Jacob said, taking hold of his arm, "sit up. Warm up."

Brian accepted the man's help and saw they were in a small room. Most of the near wall was taken up by a large fireplace. Several logs burned brightly in the iron grate and threw out a continuous heat. Brian shivered again, flexed his hands and his feet and rubbed the tip of his nose.

"Don't think we're hurt too bad," Jacob said, leaning against the wall. "Sure as hell didn't feel good, though."

Brian nodded. He held his hands out to the fire, and then he rubbed them together. After a minute, he looked at Jacob and said, "This place sucks."

Jacob let out a laugh and grinned. "You're damned right it does."

Brian thought for a moment before he asked, "Did you bring me in here?"

"No," Jacob said. "I thought you brought us in here."

"Not me," Brian said. "So, did you start the fire?"

"Nope," Jacob said.

Brian frowned. "I thought I saw a friend of mine in the freezing room. But I figured it was just my head reacting to everything. And if it was, where did he go?"

Brian looked around the room and saw there was a door to the left and to the right.

And the door to the right opened.

John stepped into the room, and behind him was a man who had to duck to enter the room. He was thin, his face sharp and his cheekbones well-defined. He wore a long black cloak, over robes of soft gray and his smile stopped well short of his green eyes.

"Brian Roy," the man said, his voice deep and powerful. "Such a pleasure to meet you. I had hoped to find you earlier, in the cannibal's room, but alas, you slipped away. I did, however, find John there. Dead, of course. But he has been ever so helpful."

Brian glanced at John, but the man's face was impassive.

"I am Josephus Wahlen," the tall man said, "and I am curious who brought you here into this room. And I, especially, would like to know how he was able to light a fire. No one has ever succeeded in doing that before."

The door to the left opened suddenly, and Leo looked in.

"Hello, Brian Roy!" he said excitedly, and then he closed the door again.

Everyone in the room was silent.

A moment later, the door opened once more. But it wasn't Leo standing there.

It was Jenny. Behind her, Brian saw Shane, and slightly to Shane's right was Leo. But it was Jenny that Brian's eyes found. Her pants were soaking wet, her feet covered with a thick layer of mud.

And she had a pump-action shotgun.

Josephus smiled at her and laughed with pleasure.

"Ah!" Josephus said, looking over at Brian. "Is this your wife, dear Jenny?"

Before he could answer, Jenny spoke up.

"Yes," she said coldly. "I am his dear wife."

The weapon roared twice, the sounds deafening in the confines of the small room.

Both John and Josephus vanished, the ghosts' screams of rage were louder than the shotgun's blasts.

CHAPTER 44
SURPRISED

It had been over a century since he had experienced pain. His thoughts were as scattered as his form. When he finally pulled himself together, he stood in the main crypt.

Josephus seethed with rage and caught sight of John, who lay on the floor with a stunned expression on his face. With a howl, Josephus reached down, grabbed hold of John and lifted the spirit into the air. John tried to twist free, but Josephus held on tight. Glaring at the man, Josephus began draining John's energy.

John's agonized shrieks were a poor substitute for what Josephus really wanted.

Suddenly, the fog began to thicken, making it difficult for them to get away. The fog was his; both to control and to hunt in.

And he would go hunting.

Josephus continued to push until he knew the fog smothered the cemetery and the marsh. When he was finished, he turned his attention to John once more.

The man was attempting to crawl away, dragging himself forward.

Josephus smiled, moved forward and caught hold of John's upper body. With a sigh, he slowly began to scalp John, the man's screams pleasing to Josephus' ears.

CHAPTER 45
TROUBLE AHEAD

"Oh," Leo said and came to a stop.

Jenny accidentally ran through him, cold shocking her body. She twisted around in the fog, the shotgun still held tightly in her hands. "What do you mean, 'Oh'?"

Leo looked to the left, and then to the right. He frowned. "This is not good."

Brian untied himself from the man and stood by her, resting a shaking hand on her shoulder. He leaned forward, kissed her and said, "Thank you."

"Oh Jesus, Brian, are you okay?" she asked.

He nodded and Jenny smiled with relief, as warmth and affection flooded through her. "I love you."

"Love you, too, babe," he said, smiling.

She saw the lines of care and fear etched into his face. His eyes were sunken slightly, and he looked older. The stranger who was with him looked even worse and smelled horrible. Like someone who hadn't bathed in years.

Don't judge, Jenny told herself.

Brian looked over at Shane, extended his hand and said, "Thank you."

Shane gave him a tight grin, shook it and said, "Who's your friend?"

"Jacob," the man said. He looked around and said, "This fog is thicker than usual."

"That is why I said 'Oh,' " Leo said. "We may have some difficulty returning to the entrance."

Jenny stared at him for a minute, and then she said in a sharp tone, "I thought you said you could get us out when we came in?"

"I can," Leo said, smiling. "It will be difficult, though. It seems as though the fog has been both thickened and lengthened. We may have quite a trip ahead of ourselves."

"But we can still get out?" Shane asked.

"Of course," Leo smiled.

"How long?" Jacob asked.

"That is difficult to say," Leo said, frowning. "Possibly several days."

"*Days?*" Jenny asked, trying to keep the anger out of her voice.

"Yes," Leo said, oblivious to her tone. "In fact, I suspect we may have to deal with additional ghosts as we make our way towards the exit. I fear they will be rather intent on stopping us."

"Yeah," Jacob said, "you've got that right, kid."

"Ghosts in the fog?" Brian asked.

Jenny nodded. "I met one; a little girl named Ruth."

"She's okay," Jacob said. "I've spoken to Ruth a bit over the years. But there are others. They're not as pleasant or as helpful as Ruth. Far from it."

Jenny looked at the men. Brian and Jacob were worn and tired. Shane adjusted his knuckle-dusters.

They're waiting for me, Jenny realized in surprise. *They're waiting for me to make a decision.*

She straightened up slightly. "Okay. Leo, lead the way. We need to leave as quickly as we can."

"Yes, Jennifer Roy," Leo said, "you are absolutely correct."

Leo led the way, and Jenny stayed close to her husband.

She wasn't going to lose him again.

CHAPTER 46

SEARCHING FOR HIS PREY

The world in which Josephus Wahlen lived was a strange one. Even after more than a century within its confines, he still didn't know all of the curious physical laws. He knew, for instance, about Brian Roy. Rumors of a man who could see the dead, a rare occurrence, rippled through the shadow world.

Josephus' curiosity had been piqued, and he had wished to meet Brian.

And how fortuitous he had been when Brian had become the caretaker of Wood's Cemetery.

Yet Josephus' prey was in danger of slipping away.

Josephus wished to fight the man. To challenge someone who had wreaked such havoc upon the spirits. Josephus had not had any worthy entertainment in decades.

Brian could not be allowed to get away.

Nor would Josephus ignore the insult Jenny had made by shooting him.

He bristled at the memory and turned his attention back to the crypt. The dead from the crypt had gathered around him.

All of them.

He could feel their fear as it pulsed off of them.

Josephus smiled, and they all moved back as far as they could. Each and every man, woman, and child feared him.

"You will go into the fog," Josephus said.

The ghosts glanced at one another, uncomfortably. Going out was dangerous. Some of them had become trapped there, gone mad, their pained shrieks audible at times when the fog was thick. The crypt was neither joyful nor free of fear, but it was better, far better than the alternative.

"You will hunt down the living in there," Josephus continued. "For each one you bring to me alive, I shall ignore you for a century."

Many of them had felt Josephus' wrath. Being ignored by Josephus was as close to heaven as the dead in the crypt could hope.

Josephus smiled at their excitement. Then he let the smile fall away.

"Find them," Josephus said, his voice hard and cold. "Find them, or you will all suffer."

He turned, faced the door and threw his will against it.

The locks shattered and the door sprang back. Beyond the world was gray.

The dead raced past him to begin their hunt.

Josephus' smile returned as he thought of how he would torture Jenny and her husband.

CHAPTER 47
BRIAN GETS WET

Brian was tired. Physically exhausted, his muscles aching and his head pounding. But he powered through it all. He had to.

They walked at a slow pace. They traveled through the water, solid ground being rare and hard to find. He could smell the stink of swamp mud with every step, and he wondered how long it would be before they found a way out.

When they came to a small patch of ground, which rose up a little above the waterline, Leo gestured for them to gather upon it.

"What is it, Leo?" Brian asked, wincing as he dropped down to sit.

"Something has changed," Leo said. "Do you feel it?"

Brian and the others looked around. He and Jenny shook their heads.

"It feels colder, doesn't it," Shane said as he nodded.

Leo nodded. "Yes, Shane Ryan, you are absolutely correct. It does feel colder, although it is not by much. We must assume, then, that the dead have found their way into the fog."

"How many dead?" Jenny asked, putting two fresh rounds into the shotgun.

"I am not certain," Leo said.

"Can you guess?" she asked.

Leo closed his eyes, concentrated and then he opened them and smiled. "Yes."

Brian sighed. "How many, Leo?"

"Three to four hundred dead," Leo said, nodding. "At least three hundred. It is why the temperature has changed."

"Three to four hundred," Brian murmured.

"Yes, at least," Leo said, nodding. "I will go and investigate. Please stay here until I return."

Before anyone could stop him, Leo left.

The four of them sat and looked at one another.

"He's dead," Jacob said.

"Yeah," Brian said.

"Was he that queer before dying?" Jacob asked. Both Shane and Jenny looked at him, shock on their faces. "What?"

Brian quickly explained about Jacob, and the shocked looks fell away. Jacob turned to him and said, "What did I say?"

"The word 'queer,' " Brian said. "It's derogatory slang for a homosexual."

"Oh," Jacob said, nodding. "Okay, then. Well, no, I was just wondering if he was strange."

"Yes," Jenny said, resting the shotgun on her lap. "Oh yes."

"Good guy, though," Shane said. "Really came through for us before."

Brian nodded his agreement. "Guy's a lot stronger than he looks."

"Not doubting it," Jacob said. He pulled at his beard and looked around nervously.

"You okay?" Brian asked him.

"Don't know," Jacob said. "Feels strange out here. Different. Usually, when I look behind me, the door is back there. It's not anymore. If we get separated, I'll be lost."

"We'll wait here for Leo," Jenny said. "He'll be able to lead us out."

"I hope like hell you're right," Jacob said. He cracked his knuckles.

Brian didn't like the idea of being trapped in the fog either.

And if there are a few hundred more dead out here, Brian thought with a sigh, *then they're probably coming for us.*

"You okay, babe?" Jenny asked.

Brian smiled at her. "Yeah, I'm good. Just worried."

She nodded. "Me too."

"You were pretty fantastic," he added after a moment.

Jenny grinned. "Felt good to pull the trigger."

"I bet," Brian said.

"Josephus," Jacob said, shaking his head. "Terrible creature. Can't imagine what he was like when he was alive."

"I don't even want to think about that," Shane said. He fished out his cigarettes and lit one.

Jacob's eyes lit up. "Hey, can I get one of those?"

Shane nodded, shook out a second one and passed it and the lighter over.

Jacob's hands trembled as he put the cigarette in his mouth and managed to light it. He closed his eyes, inhaled deeply, let out a racking cough as he exhaled and grinned. He passed the lighter back, saying, "Thanks. Been a long time since I had a whole cigarette."

"Terrible," Shane said sympathetically.

Leo appeared from the fog. He looked concerned.

"Leo," Jenny said. "What's going on?"

"Unfortunately, there are nearly four hundred ghosts here," Leo said. "And they are actively looking for you. All of you in general, and in particular they are searching for you, Jenny."

Jenny paled slightly. "Me?"

Leo nodded. "Oh yes. It seems you angered Josephus when you shot him."

"He deserved it," Jacob said around the cigarette, slapping at some ashes which landed in his beard.

"Undeniably," Leo agreed. "However, he is rather intent on revenge."

"What do you suggest?" Shane asked.

"We should avoid being caught," Leo replied.

"Can we get out?" Brian asked.

Everyone looked at Leo.

"Of course," Leo said.

"Alive?" Jenny asked.

"We have an excellent chance of getting out of here alive," Leo said.

Brian shook his head. "Okay, Leo. What do we need to do?"

"Follow me," Leo said, and he turned away. They all scrambled off the small dry patch, splashed into the still water, and followed him as quickly as they could.

Faintly, Brian heard whispers. Once more, he and the others formed a single line, with Leo at the head and Shane at the back. Jacob smoked happily, flicking the butt off to the side when he finished it. Brian could see shapes in the fog, and he knew they were getting closer. They weren't the curious abominations which had chased him and John through Wood's Cemetery.

A huge hand lashed out of the fog and tried to grab Brian's forearm. A face appeared. Gruesome, pox ridden. Sores around the mouth and nose, flesh hanging in strips from the man's cheeks. Brian could see where teeth should have been, a swollen, wormlike tongue twisting in the ghost's mouth.

Brian brought his right hand up and smashed the ghost in the face. The iron connected and the ghost vanished. Jenny pumped a round into the chamber of the shotgun.

"Hold your fire," Shane said softly. "It'll just bring the rest running."

Brian glanced at Jenny and saw her loosen her finger on the trigger.

"Wait," Leo said, and he vanished.

They stood still and listened.

Several high-pitched shrieks filled the air, and a flash rippled through the fog.

"What the hell?" Jacob asked, looking around.

Leo reappeared, his face paler than usual.

"Come," Leo said with some effort. "We must continue."

"Leo," Brian said. "What happened?"

Leo gave him a small smile. "There were a dozen or so of them. I had to expend a great deal of energy to disperse them. They would have taken me otherwise."

"You don't want to be brought to Josephus," Jacob said softly.

"No," Leo said. "I most certainly do not."

Once more, Leo led, and they followed.

CHAPTER 48
NO SYMPATHY

Josephus, when he had been alive, had been quite adept at feigning sympathy. This was how he had been able to obtain a position as a pastor. How he had been able to convince young girls to trust him. Sympathy had been an effective tool to aid in his hunting.

Being dead, Josephus no longer had a need to pretend. He had undeniable power and control over the afterlife, which the residents of the cemetery and the crypt found themselves in.

He was a harsh and cruel god.

Failure was met with instant and brutal punishment.

With the challenge of the living in his domain, Josephus was even more brutal. When Guy Wetherbee appeared, all six foot six of his pox ridden flesh, Josephus had never hesitated. He had shredded the man's spirit, littering the floor of the crypt with Guy's remains. The man would serve as an abject lesson to any who returned without the prize Josephus demanded.

And they began to come back quickly.

First, nearly a dozen of them. Then in ones and twos. They were shocked, numbed and surprised at their defeat.

Josephus gave them no time to explain. He didn't care. He wanted results, not reasons and certainly not excuses.

Fortunately for the crypt dwellers, none of them attempted to explain. It would have resulted in decades of torment. It was far better, they knew, to accept their punishment submissively. The quicker the punishment was done, the sooner they could hide and weather out this new storm of Josephus'.

Or so they thought.

As he finished shredding a pair of young twins, Josephus caught sight of Wetherbee. The poxy ghost staggered forward, and Josephus grabbed him.

"Back into the fog, wretch!" he yelled, and he hurled the man through the open door.

There would be no refuge from this storm.

Each cast back to the crypt would be sent once again after the living.

A flicker of motion caught Josephus' eye and he turned in time to see Brian's one-time traveling companion, John, stand up.

"Get out," Josephus hissed. "Into the fog with you, and find them."

John hesitated for a moment, and then he hurried past Josephus and out into the cemetery.

Josephus ached suddenly.

The effort it took to keep the fog in place was tremendous. He wouldn't be able to continue doing it indefinitely. If Josephus were to withdraw the fog, any of the dead not in the crypt would be trapped in the marsh.

And it would also mean Brian and his hateful wife would have gotten away.

Away.

The thought enraged Josephus, and he waited impatiently for his wishes to be fulfilled.

CHAPTER 49

TRYING TO GET OUT

Shane kept pace with the others, his hand tired from the steady grip he was forced to keep on the knuckle-dusters.

The dead were attacking more often.

He had struck down three of them, and Brian another two. Jacob was unarmed, yet he was skillful enough to avoid the arms of the dead. Jenny had taken down four of them, and not with the shotgun. With the iron ring, on her right hand, she had beaten the ghosts down with powerful blows. The woman was definitely capable of handling herself.

Leo would occasionally dispatch some, then he would have them stop, and he would slip away. The curious light would flash, and the strange little man would return, looking worse than before. Whatever Leo was doing, Shane realized, it was taking a lot out of him.

We're all tired, Shane thought. His legs were cold, and they ached. His boots felt as though they weighed a hundred pounds each and his pants seemed to have been cut from concrete. Occasionally, Shane's stomach growled, but he ignored its rumbles as best he could.

We'll be done soon, he told himself, unsure whether he was telling himself the truth or a pretty lie. *Make some nice hot coffee, give it a good shot of brandy, and drink it down as quickly as you can.* Shane smiled, picturing the steaming mug.

And then the image was shattered.

Dozens of ghosts swarmed out of the fog. Within a heartbeat, he found himself fighting for his life. He struck the dead repeatedly.

Brian was swinging wildly and Leo was battling five of the dead at once.

Jenny destroyed another with a vicious backhand, brought the shotgun up and had the weapon knocked from her grasp by a teenage girl.

Horrified, Shane watched the weapon spin away, and get snatched out of the air by Jacob.

Everyone, living and dead, paused to look at the ragged, thin man.

Jacob smiled at all of them. He brought the shotgun up to his shoulder with one smooth, fluid motion. After the first shot, while the red shell casing spun lazily through the air in a loose arc, the battle began anew.

But it was too late for the dead.

Shane turned his full attention to the ghosts who tried to drag him down. With his attention focused on them, he couldn't spare a glance to his friends, but he heard the shotgun. It roared again.

The dead were gone.

Shane looked at Jacob, who still had the weapon at his shoulder. The look on the man's face was grim and hard. It was a killer's face, the expression of a man who had fought long and dirty for his life, and had always come out on top. Jacob slowly lowered the weapon, then he handed it over to Jenny.

"Thanks," she said.

Jacob nodded, pulled at his beard and smiled. "Well, guess we best be on our way."

"Yes," Leo said. "It would be wise. I am afraid the noise of the shotgun probably alerted the dead to our exact location. They, like us, have difficulty navigating the fog. But with the firing to act as a beacon, they will be here shortly."

"Leo," Brian said. "Are you alright?"

"No, Brian Roy," Leo said tiredly. "I am not. If I must exert myself any more, I will be forced to retire for a short time in order to recuperate my strength."

"How much is a short time?" Jenny asked.

Leo smiled nervously. "I am unsure, Jennifer Roy. It may only be a few hours. Or perhaps weeks."

"Well," Brian said, "let's just make it out of here."

"Alright," Leo said. He turned to lead again, and Jenny reloaded the shotgun.

A shape came out of the fog towards them, approaching Leo. Shane tightened his grip on the knuckle-dusters even as Jenny chambered a round. Leo stiffened.

When the figure came close enough to be fully visible, Shane saw it was a woman, perhaps the same age as himself. Then he heard Jenny gasp, the weapon dropping slightly in her hands.

"Oh my God," Brian said.

"No, Brian," the woman said, smiling. "It's just me, Sylvia."

CHAPTER 50

THE RETURN OF AN OLD FRIEND

Jenny nearly dropped the shotgun into the marsh water, and she wanted to give Sylvia a hug. Neither action would have worked out well. They still needed the shotgun, and Jenny was fairly certain that she would go right through her.

Instead, she reached out, found Brian's hand and squeezed it tightly.

Leo smiled, walked to Sylvia, and rested his head against her arm.

"You're in a bad place," Sylvia said, "in case you guys haven't figured it out yet on your own."

"No," Brian said, shaking his head. "We got the memo."

"Good," Sylvia said. "We're not far from the exit. Even with this creature controlling the fog, I know the way back."

"How did you get here?" Jenny asked. "I didn't think you had left Nashua."

"The fog leads into the shadow world, and I've been fortunate enough to have Leo show me the path," Sylvia said, smiling.

Sylvia turned to Leo and said, "If you push now, I'll help you."

"Alright," Leo said softly.

"Push what?" Jacob said, asking Jenny's own question.

Sylvia smiled. "Watch."

She interlaced her fingers with Leo's and held onto him. Jenny watched as both Sylvia and Leo closed their eyes. A curious, electric feeling spread out from them, and it was followed by a pulse. It rippled outward, pushing the fog back.

Screams erupted from the marsh and the hairs on Jenny's neck stood on end. She held onto Brian and the shotgun tighter and stared at the small passage Leo and Sylvia had created. Perhaps fifty or sixty feet ahead, Jenny caught sight of the old pickup truck they had climbed through to get into the fog.

They were just a few steps away.

Sylvia held onto Leo and led the way, power radiating from her. Shadows lurked within the fog on either side of the tunnel Sylvia had created, yet they didn't try to reach through. They just hung back, seemingly afraid.

Jenny kept a firm grip on the shotgun, though, and she looked from left to right and back again. Shane kept pace behind her, and Brian and Jacob stumbled in front of her. When they were nearly half way to the truck, somebody stepped out of the fog.

It was a middle-aged woman, her face fat and puffy, and her clothes were plain and simple. She tried to step around Sylvia, reaching out for Jacob.

Sylvia made a small gesture with her free hand, and the woman shrieked.

Jenny watched in horror as the ghost was turned inside out, its screams of pain and horror vanishing after a moment. The sounds seemed to be swallowed up by the fog.

The other ghosts, who lined the path, stepped back until they were no longer visible.

Within a matter of moments, they were only ten feet away from the truck, and Jenny's heart thumped erratically in her chest.

"Just keep moving forward," Shane said softly. "Don't think about anything else. Don't worry about anything else. Just walk."

Jenny nodded.

She watched as Leo passed into the cab and Sylvia took up a position on the right of the open door. Then Jacob and Brian, and finally Jenny went through. She scrambled across the old, rotten bench seat, and out the other side.

Cold descended upon her instantly, and Brian helped her. A bit of fog clung to the truck, but above them. The night sky was dark and beautiful. There was no moon, only the light of the stars shining down on the marsh.

Shane appeared a moment later, and then Sylvia.

Jenny looked to her dead friend, and Sylvia smiled.

"How?" Jenny asked. "How are you so strong?"

"It's not that I am so strong," Sylvia said, "but they're so weak. Josephus feeds off of their energy, what little of it they are able to muster. If he didn't siphon their power, Leo and I would never have been able to stop the attacks, let alone beat them."

"Oh," Jenny said. "Wow."

"We have to go, though, but I'll see you soon, Jenny," Sylvia said. Then she took Leo's hand and the two ghosts slipped away into the night.

Jenny looked to Brian, and he smiled at her. Jacob stood on the other side, nose wrinkled.

"Christ almighty," Jacob said.

"What?" Shane asked.

"Is it the marsh that smells so bad, or is this what America smells like now?" Jacob asked.

Jenny laughed, surprised at the comment.

"No," Brian said, "pretty sure it's the marsh."

"Fair enough," Jacob said. He looked around, eyes darting everywhere. He grinned, most of his teeth missing, the others stained with age and lack of care. "So, where the hell can I get a cold beer?"

"My house," Brian said. "And we can all get a shower there, too."

"A shower," Jacob said, his voice dropping to a whisper. "An honest to goodness shower."

Jenny reached out, took Brian's hand, and said, "Let's get the hell out of here."

Brian nodded, and the four of them headed towards a street light in the distance.

CHAPTER 51

A SETBACK

Anger flared within him, and Josephus fumed in silence.

"They're gone," a voice whispered.

Josephus glanced down, and he saw Ruth. The little girl smiled at him wickedly.

"Gone," she said again, and she vanished.

And he knew it was true.

Brian and his thrice damned wife! Josephus thought, snarling. *They're all gone. Each and every one of them.*

Enraged, Josephus finally let go of his grip upon the fog. It collapsed upon itself, the force of it rippling through the crypt. The agony of those caught beyond the iron fence, washed over him. They had failed him, and therefore they would suffer until he expanded the fog again. They would be trapped and alone, unable to find one another, or anything else familiar to them.

He turned away from the crypt and made his way back to where his bones lay. They were wrapped in the rotted remains of his clothes beside the small stream. It was time to hunt Brian and Jenny down himself.

Never had Josephus attempted to reach out beyond the iron fence.

He sat down beside his earthly remains and looked hard at his skull. Wisps of black hair still clung to his skull and Josephus could remember when it fell in long locks.

Ah, he thought. The girls had loved his hair.

Until he strangled the life out of them at the end.

Josephus smiled at the pleasant memories and thought about how he would crush Brian and Jenny himself.

CHAPTER 52
THE ROY HOUSE, MAY 4TH, 2016

They had all showered, and they had all eaten.

Shane was asleep in a chair, arms folded across his chest as he snored lightly. He wore a pair of Brian's sweats and thick socks. The fire burned brightly in the parlor, throwing out warmth. Jacob Wurbach sat in Jenny's chair. He, too, was dressed in some of Brian's clothes, and they hung upon the man. But Jacob was wide awake, and he had borrowed the hair clippers, and Brian had given the man a razor and a toothbrush.

The man in Jenny's chair was not the same who had left the marsh. Jacob's hair was buzzed short, and he was clean shaven. While he was twitchy and nervous, he still had a tremendous smile on his harsh, lined face. He had enjoyed two beers, potato chips, and a bowl of cereal. Jacob had wisely stopped after the cereal.

Brian adjusted his arm, which was wrapped around Jenny. He nodded to Jacob.

"I feel strange," Jacob said.

"How so?" Brian asked.

"Like this is a dream," Jacob said, gesturing around the room. "Terrified that it is, actually."

"Yeah," Brian agreed. "Kind of worried it is, too."

"I feel like Rip Van Winkle," Jacob said after a moment. "Except I haven't been asleep. Haven't had a good time, either."

"No," Brian said. "Can't imagine you did. Have you thought about what you're going to do next?"

Jacob was quiet for a moment before he replied, "Not really. I mean, hell, I've been away for over forty years. I don't know anything about anything. And who's going to believe me if I said who I was? They'd put me in an asylum."

"They would," Brian said. "Maybe we can all talk about it in the morning and figure it out."

"I'd like to," Jacob said. He went to pull at his beard, remembered it wasn't there and smiled ruefully. "I'll have to get used to being shaved. I don't mind, though. Hated the damned thing."

Silence fell over them. The logs in the fireplace popped occasionally, and after several minutes, Brian said, "I'm going back to the cemetery in a few days."

Jacob looked at him and then asked, "Why?"

"Josephus," Brian replied. "He tried to hurt me. Pretty sure he was going to hurt Jenny, too."

Jacob nodded. "He would have. How are you going to stop him?"

"Not sure," Brian said. "I'll have to do some research on it. But I am going to stop him. That's for certain."

"Well," Jacob said, "count on me. I'd like to put him down."

"Thank you," Brian said.

Jacob grinned. "No need to thank me, Brian. You helped me get out of there. He kept me in there. Figure we both can get a little bit of revenge on Josephus Wahlen."

Jenny moved a little in Brian's embrace, and he smiled at her. Looking over to Jacob he said, "Do you want me to show you to the spare bedroom?"

"No," Jacob said, shaking his head. "Don't know if I can sleep just yet. And when I do, I'll probably stretch out in front of the fire."

"Well," Brian said, "I'm going to get my sleepy girl upstairs. If you need anything, just follow the sounds of my snores."

"Will do," Jacob said.

Brian kissed Jenny on the forehead, and gently woke her up.

CHAPTER 53
AWAKE AND IN THE KITCHEN, MAY 4TH, 2016

Jacob stood in the kitchen of Brian and Jenny's house. He had his hands on the edge of the counter and looked out the window behind the sink. He saw a large, dark shape swoop down from the night sky and land in a field. A barn owl hunting its dinner.

Jacob took a glass from the drying rack and filled it with cold water from the tap. He drank it slowly and wandered around the kitchen. The entire room was a marvel to him. The nearly silent refrigerator, the gas stove with the curious clock. The coffee maker and the toaster. So many familiar items, yet each far different than when he had been free.

He walked to the refrigerator, opened it and stared in awe at the bright light and the food arrayed neatly before him. Cold, crisp air washed over him, and he smelled a hundred different scents. Each of them tantalizing.

He smiled, reached in and plucked a grape from a bunch of them. He popped it into his mouth and bit down, the fruit, sweet and delicious. The juice was cold as it exploded against his tongue and cheek. It caused his teeth to ache, and he chuckled, closing the refrigerator door. He opened the freezer and looked at the ice cream.

His stomach rumbled, and he longed to eat the frozen desert, but he was sure he'd make himself sick if he did. Yet it was almost worth it.

He hadn't had ice cream since the day before he had become trapped in the fog. The memory of that day sent a spike of fear through his chest, and he quickly closed the freezer.

He went over to the light switch for the kitchen, flicked it up and down several times and was amazed at how quickly and silently everything worked. He wandered back to the sink and turned on the hot water. In a matter of moments, it was hot, almost to the point of being painful.

Jacob laughed, shook his head and shut the water off.

This must all be real, he thought, looking around the kitchen. *I don't have enough of an imagination to think this up.*

With another laugh, he walked over to the refrigerator and opened it again. Smiling, he looked at the bright light and all of the food before him.

CHAPTER 54

AN EPIPHANY

The water moved sluggishly through the darkness. Fish swam, and insects skirted along the surface of the cold stream. The dark settled into the bones and ate at the will to live.

Josephus remembered all of it as he sat beside his remains. In the twisted paths and lanes of his memory, he roamed, searching for a way to enact his revenge. Seeking a method by which he could punish Jenny.

A bit of doggerel, a hint of a text translated from the Latin. A single word.

And he smiled.

Possession.

CHAPTER 55
PREPPING FOR A 5K RACE, MAY 4TH, 2016

Dylan Mailer walked along the road, heading towards Wood's Cemetery. It was a good place to start his run, a spot he could fixate on after he hit the halfway point and turned around. He needed to have a goal when he ran; the cemetery's iron fence would serve the purpose admirably. Dylan knew a five-kilometer race wasn't much, but at thirty-three and out of shape, it might as well be the Boston Marathon.

He adjusted his armband with his iPhone in it, the music set up and ready to go. The new, behind-the-ear earbuds were fit snuggly in place. He reached behind him and slipped the water bottle free from its pouch at the small of his back. Dylan twisted the cap off, smelled the sharp tang of vodka, and smiled. He would hydrate when he got home. Just a good buzz to get through the initial pain.

He took several long drinks and instantly felt the burn in his stomach. It was only then that he realized he had forgotten to eat. His stomach cramped instantly, and he winced. The vodka raced through him and in a dozen steps he was close to being drunk.

In for a penny, in for a pound, he thought, and he finished off the bottle.

With a sharp right turn, he found himself approaching the cemetery and he nodded drunkenly. Clumsily, he put the bottle back into its pouch, and he wondered, briefly, if he should wait a bit before he ran.

Maybe I shouldn't run at all, he told himself. He left the asphalt of the road for the grass shoulder, made his way to the fence and sat down. He leaned back against the iron bars and closed his eyes.

His stomach rumbled and twisted, and he wondered if he would throw up. A terrible headache started at the base of his skull and worked its way forward, steadily. Dylan opened his eyes, and the edges of his vision were black. Curved lines created a tunnel, and they tightened and relaxed, repeatedly.

With a groan, he twisted to the right and vomited, the vodka and bile stinking in the green grass. Dylan tried to spit the foul taste out, but to no avail. His headache grew worse, and then he shuddered.

Hello, Dylan, a voice said.

It was a hard voice. Brutal and male. Domineering.

Dylan didn't answer.

You don't have to speak, the stranger in his head chuckled. *I suppose introductions are in order, however. My name is Josephus, but you can call me Joe. You're going to help me.*

Dylan tried to push the voice out of his head, but Joe only laughed.

Pain exploded in Dylan's abdomen, and he threw up again. For several long minutes, he leaned over, dry heaving until the agony stopped.

Sit up, Joe said. It was a command, and Dylan obeyed.

Excellent, Joe said. *You learn quickly. Now, do as I say.*

Dylan listened to Joe and nodded.

He got to his feet and staggered to the front gate and turned into the cemetery. Dylan forced himself to walk forward, the memory of the pain horribly fresh. He managed to make his way to the back of the cemetery and turn right, listening to the directions of Joe. Dylan found an open door set into a hillside, and he went in. He ignored everything in the crypt around him and headed toward a door at the back wall. It was also open, and he entered it. At the far end, he saw a small tunnel, barely visible to the left.

When Joe told him to get down and crawl into the hole, Dylan balked.

The punishment was instant and horrifically painful. His eyes watered, and his nose bled.

Dylan dropped to his knees, then got down on his belly and forced himself into the small opening. The weight of the world seemed to settle down upon him, and Dylan forced down panic. A tremendous fear of claustrophobia beat at him, yet it paled in comparison to the fear he felt for Joe.

He screamed as insects ran over him, something with a thousand legs racing across his face. He inhaled spider webs and dust. A deep cold penetrated his flesh while sharp rocks cut at his skin. He could feel himself bleeding, his clothes being torn. And still, he had to crawl on.

A little further, Joe said cheerfully. *Just a little further. This task is nearly done.*

Dylan didn't respond. He was focused on each inch he had to cover. He kept his eyelids closed, fearful of bugs. Afraid of them biting his eyes.

Joe pushed him forward relentlessly. Each time Dylan paused, another part of his body would explode with pain. Eventually, he tumbled down into an open area. He wept as fear coursed through him. Faintly, Dylan heard water and, a musky, rotten smell filled his nose. Dylan ached as he lay on cool dirt, and he numbly wondered what was next.

Joe didn't make him wait for long.

Dylan was shoved into the back of his own mind and huddled there, a mute observer as his body, under Joe's control, crawled ahead. Dylan could feel everything, the touch of the dirt, the scrape of his knees against rocks.

And his fingers as they found some smooth and curiously cool stone.

Ah, Joe said with some satisfaction. *Here are my bones.*

Within a moment, both hands were questing through Joe's bones and shortly after, Joe sighed with pleasure.

Yes, Joe said, *this should do quite nicely, I believe.*

Dylan felt the man pick up a small finger bone with one of Dylan's hands.

Open wide, Dylan, Joe said, chuckling.

Dylan fought to keep his mouth closed, but he couldn't. Joe was too strong. He felt his jaw shift down, his lips open and his teeth part. Joe forced Dylan's tongue to extend, and the bone was placed on the back of it, just like a pill. A bitter, foul pill.

Tears fell freely down Dylan's face as Joe made him swallow, and bone burned his throat as it made its rough passage to his stomach.

Dylan's consciousness was slammed backward, and Joe took over completely. As Joe turned his body around to return the way it had come, Dylan cowered in a corner of his mind.

Not real, Dylan thought desperately. *Not real. Not real. Not real. Not real.*

Beneath his litany, he heard Joe laugh, and he felt his flesh scrape against stone.

CHAPTER 56

BREAKFAST WITH THE CREW, MAY 4TH, 2016

Brian worked on his third cup of coffee while Shane finished another shot of whiskey. The man drank the liquor like a fish, and Brian wondered why.

Jacob sat on the back steps. Brian had given him a cigar, and the rich tobacco smoke drifted into the kitchen through the screen door. It was a good smell. And the man, so far out of time and place, was happy.

"How many eggs did he eat?" Shane asked.

"Eight," Brian said. "Told me they tasted even better than he remembered."

"Damn," Shane said, shaking his head. "Eight?"

"Yeah," Brian said, grinning. "Finished off half a rack of bacon, too. Plus, a whole pot of coffee. Thought for sure he'd pop."

"Still might," Shane said with a smile. "That cigar might do the trick."

Brian chuckled. "True. Very true."

"So," Shane said, his voice becoming serious, "when do you want to take care of Mr. Josephus Wahlen?"

"Just as soon as I can figure out how to do it," Brian said. "I don't want to try and bind him. I want him destroyed. Completely."

"Sounds good to me," Shane said. "From what I could see, he was bad news."

Brian could only nod. He had a sudden urge to drink and to light up a cigar. But didn't succumb to the desire. Jenny would be too upset with him. Especially after everything she had gone through to help him.

"You okay?" Shane asked.

"Yeah," Brian said. "Just frustrated with everything."

"We'll take care of it," Shane said. "We'll take care of all of it. Don't worry."

"Thanks," Brian said. He drank the rest of his coffee, considered a fourth cup and then pushed the mug away from him. Too much caffeine wouldn't be good for him either.

The back door opened, and Jacob walked in, smiling broadly. He winced slightly, paused, and then came the rest of the way into the kitchen.

"You alright?" Shane asked.

"Little bit of indigestion," Jacob said. He pulled a chair out and sat down at the table. "Still want to eat everything I see."

"Don't think your stomach would appreciate that," Brian said.

"No," Jacob agreed. "I would still enjoy the hell out of the meal, though."

A loud squeak sounded from the ceiling and both Jacob and Shane looked up.

"The shower," Brian said. "Makes a racket when you turn it off."

"Didn't notice last night," Shane said.

"Neither did I," Jacob said, chuckling.

Brian smiled at the two men and realized he felt safe. He looked at Shane and Jacob and asked, "Either of you want more coffee?"

CHAPTER 57

RUNNELS RIDGE ROAD, MAY 4TH, 2016

Neal Lars served as Mont Vernon's part-time policeman, and it was a job he loved. He had spent most of his childhood as the butt of other people's jokes. Neal had filled out, in both height and weight after high school, and after a few years on a lobster boat out of Bar Harbor, the weight had become muscle. He had taken a few night classes in criminal justice, gotten his associates degree, and then he had landed the Mont Vernon job.

Granted, it was only part-time, and the rest of his income was supplemented as a delivery man for the MV Lumber Yard, but he got to wear a badge. The gun wasn't anything to him. He'd had a license to 'carry concealed' since he was twenty-one.

Neal liked to use his hands. They were rough and calloused from years of hauling lumber, and he enjoyed locking his fingers around a perpetrator's wrist. He knew how to apply just enough pressure with his thumb to bring a big man down to the ground.

And nothing, absolutely *nothing* was as much fun as when he got to do it to someone who had picked on him. More often than not, they didn't recognize him. His face was broader, and he had grown a thick, dark brown mustache. Lars was a common name in the area as well, so there wasn't anyone who would have associated him with the skinny little runt they had all bullied in school.

Neal remembered them all. Every, single, one.

The weekend before, Neal had even gotten a hold of Jeff Perkins. Perkins had tormented Neal all the way from the third to the sixth grade. Perkins had moved out of the area, down to Boston and started up a law firm after college.

Perkins' mother, who had been a sweet lady, had died. He was up for the funeral and gotten a little drunk at the Leap Café. Neal had waited two hours in the parking lot for Perkins to stumble out of the bar. Arrested him on the spot for public drunkenness. Perkins had even swung at Neal. A shame, too. Perkins had been forced to have his eyes flushed out after a good dose of pepper spray.

Neal was thinking fondly on the arrest when he caught sight of a man walking strangely down the side of the road. The man was dressed in expensive running clothes, but he was filthy, covered not only in dirt and mud, but what looked like blood, as well. When Neal passed by him, the man looked like he was in shock.

Neal flipped on his hazards, pulled over to the side of the road and took his portable radio down from the dashboard.

"State Dispatch, this is Officer Neal Lars in Mont Vernon."

"Go ahead, Officer Lars," a man responded. "This is dispatch."

"Could you send an ambulance to one-zero-zero Runnels Ridge Road, I've got a pedestrian who looks like he took a fall somewhere," Neal said. "Going to talk to him now."

"Copy, Officer Lars," the dispatcher said. "We'll send an ambulance your way. You in your patrol car?"

"Negative," Neal said. "Got the delivery truck. Hazards on."

"Good, copy. Dispatch out."

Neal put the radio back and got out of the truck.

The battered man continued to walk, weaving slightly as he did so.

"Sir," Neal said, smiling. "Sir, are you okay?"

The man stopped, returned Neal's smile and said, "Why yes. Yes, I am. Why do you ask?"

"You look like you may have fallen down," Neal said, taking a cautious step towards the stranger. "What's your name?"

The man blinked, his smile faltering briefly before he said, "Dylan."

"Dylan," Neal said, walking a little closer. "My name is Officer Lars. I'd like you to take a seat on the side of the road here, okay? I'd like to have an ambulance check you out."

Dylan looked confused, his head tilted to the right.

Looks like he's listening to someone, Neal thought. He hadn't seen a blue-tooth in the man's ear.

After a moment, Dylan said, "I am not in need of medical assistance.

Please, allow me to continue on."

Another step towards Dylan showed Neal the man's eyes. The pupils fluctuated rapidly, growing and shrinking at an astonishing pace.

Something's wrong here, Neal thought. He reached down and loosened his can of pepper spray in its holster.

"Dylan," Neal said, keeping his voice low and relaxed. "I really need you to sit down now."

Dylan smiled and said, "No."

Even as Neal began to pull the pepper spray free, Dylan leaped forward, smashing a fist squarely into Neal's nose. Neal staggered back, pain exploding in his head and his eyes tearing up instantly. Blood poured down from both nostrils and Neal instantly knew the punch had broken his nose. His vision was blurry as he got the pepper spray free, but a second punch landed on his bicep and caused his arm to go numb. A third blow crashed into his solar plexus, and Neal crashed to the asphalt.

Gasping for breath, he tried to sit up, but Dylan kicked him in the head. The world went black, and Neal heard Dylan step over him. Pain dominated his thoughts as the truck's engine roared into life.

CHAPTER 58

FORCED INTO ACTION

Do it! Josephus screamed, battering Dylan's cowering spirit.

Timidly, the man crept forward to take partial control of his own body.

Where? Dylan whispered.

Josephus hesitated, dug through his memories and searched for what he had heard of Brian Roy.

Can you find someone named Roy? Josephus snapped after a moment.

Yes, Dylan said.

Then do it, Josephus commanded. He settled back and watched with a small amount of interest as Dylan operated the traveling machine.

Josephus moved excitedly within Dylan's small mind, and smiled, eager to find Brian.

CHAPTER 59
AT THE ROY RESIDENCE, 9:00 AM, MAY 4TH, 2016

"I think I found something," Brian said.

Jenny came into his small office. "What?"

Brian looked up from his computer. "Little bit of folklore here. It's shown up on a couple different websites. We have to find Josephus' remains."

Jenny frowned. "What do we do when we have them?"

"Salt them and burn them," Brian answered. "Once they're burned, and we scatter the ashes, he won't be able to manifest in our world again."

"Really?" she asked.

"Well," Brian said, sighing, "we won't know for sure if the lore's true until we do it."

"How the hell do we find out where his remains are?" Jenny said.

Jacob and Shane walked to the doorway and looked in.

"Who's remains?" Shane asked.

"Josephus'," Brian said, and he quickly repeated what he had read.

"I know where they are," Jacob said after a moment.

Everyone looked at the man.

He smiled harshly. "Spent a lot of time wandering around. They're by a stream that cuts through the hill. Hell of a hard place to get to. You have to crawl on your belly for a while to reach it. I can get there. But the three of you, you're all a little too sturdy."

"Fine with me," Jenny said. "I've got no desire to try and crawl through a tunnel to find his bones."

"It's not a tunnel," Jacob said. "Just a little passage. And it's dark as all hell. The only reason I know they're his is because the ghost of a young girl told me. We'll need to bring a light, and probably a bag. Don't want to burn the cave down with me inside."

Brian nodded. "I'm sure we have everything we need right here. And if we don't, we'll stop at a store."

"Do you hear something?" Shane asked, turning towards the window.

Brian listened closely, and he heard the sound of an engine. A big old Hemi, if the rumble was any indication.

Jenny walked over, pulled the curtain back and said, "There's a white pickup truck out at the end of the driveway." She let the fabric go and turned back to Brian. "Probably lost."

"Just so long as they're not selling anything," Brian said. "Anyway, where were we?"

"Getting what we need to roast Josephus' bones," Jacob said.

"Right," Brian said, nodding. "Let's figure all of that out ahead of time."

The others gathered around the desk, and together they began to work on a plan.

CHAPTER 60

NEAL'S TRUCK, 9:05 AM, MAY 4TH, 2016

Josephus had shoved Dylan back into a dark corner; the man's simpering was far too annoying to deal with. Josephus didn't need him anymore. He had watched the way the man had operated the 'truck,' and he knew what to do. At least for the purpose he had in mind.

All Josephus had to do was step on the right pedal, hold onto the 'steering wheel' and aim the truck to where he wanted to go.

He would have no need for the left pedal.

He wasn't going to stop.

As he waited at the end of the driveway, he saw a curtain drawn away from a window, and then put back into place.

They believed him to be in Wood's Cemetery. In the Paupers' Crypt, to be exact.

Josephus smiled. He would enjoy their surprise, almost as much as he would relish their horror when he had them. The thought of it sent a thrill through him, and Dylan's body reacted the way Josephus' own flesh had, long ago. Before his imprisonment.

Anger flared at the memory, and he fought to retain control of himself.

He would punish them soon enough. Perhaps, if he was lucky, he might even get his hands upon the wretch Jacob, who had avoided him for so many years.

Josephus looked at the house and decided where he would strike.

CHAPTER 61

GUESTS ARRIVE, 9:10 AM, MAY 4TH, 2016

"Hello."

Jenny dropped her coffee mug and bit back a curse as it shattered on the floor.

Thankfully, it was empty. Unlike the kitchen, which now had Leo standing by the pantry. His form seemed much thinner. Jenny could see through him easier than usual.

"Leo," Jenny said, taking the dustpan and brush out of the cabinet below the sink. "How are you?"

"Tired," Leo said, a confused look on his face. "And I am not quite certain how I can be tired."

"Why not?" she asked, getting down on her knees to sweep shards of the mug out from under the cabinet's overhang.

"I am dead," Leo replied. "Therefore, I should not be tired. Then again, it does raise the entire question of how I exist outside of life, as we know it."

Jenny was going to cut him off, but she didn't have to. Sylvia appeared, and she quieted Leo with a hand on his shoulder.

"Hello, Sylvia," Jenny said, smiling up at her.

Sylvia returned the smile and said, "Hello, Jenny. I'm sorry Leo scared you."

"I'm just surprised I can still be scared," Jenny said. She cleaned up the last of the broken mug, stood up and threw the remains out. She put the dustpan and brush away and looked at Sylvia. "I'm glad you came by."

"It's not a social visit, I'm afraid," Sylvia said sadly. "I can't stay very long. I used a lot of my strength yesterday. But there's something wrong. We went back to the cemetery this morning."

"And Josephus Wahlen is not there," Leo said. "He has left the place."

"What?" Jenny said, looking from one ghost to the other. "Hold on. Let me get everyone else."

"No time," Sylvia said, her form fading in and out rapidly. "Listen, we think he may have managed to possess someone."

"What?" Jenny asked, horrified. "What do you mean by possess?"

"He has taken over someone's body," Leo said.

"Why?" Jenny asked.

"We think he might be looking for Brian," Sylvia said. "You need to be careful. Both of you. We'll let you know where he is as soon as we can. Just be safe, Jenny."

As Jenny nodded, both Sylvia and Leo shimmered, and then they vanished.

Jenny suddenly became aware of the noise of her own heart, the way it thudded in her chest. Her vision blurred for a moment, then returned to normal. She felt a sickening fear and she hurried out of the kitchen.

She ran to the study and found all three men still there. Brian was in his chair, Shane sat by the desk and Jacob stood against the near wall, arms folded over his chest. Each of them looked to her, smiles on their faces.

Whatever expression they saw on her face caused the joy to leave theirs.

"Babe," Brian said, standing up quickly. "What's wrong?"

Before she could answer, an explosion of sound ripped through the air and the house shook. Jenny could hear breaking glass and shattering wood.

And mixed in with it, the roaring of an engine.

"The truck," she said, but no one heard her.

Brian was up and out of his chair as Shane and Jacob raced past her, Brian followed a moment later. Jenny stood there, alone and stunned.

Then one word leaped into her mind.

Possession.

Instead of turning to leave the study, she ran to Brian's desk.

CHAPTER 62

HELP ARRIVES, 9:15 AM, MAY 4TH, 2016

Neal realized he must have blacked out.

Cindy Ford was kneeling beside him, prying open his right eye and checking his pupils.

"Hey there, Neal," she said, smiling down at him and speaking in the professional tone he had heard more than once. "Can you tell me what happened?"

It took him a moment, but Neal finally gathered his thoughts and told her.

She nodded, looked across from him to Timmy White, who slipped a pressure cuff around Neal's bicep.

"Okay, Neal," she said, still smiling, "you know the drill. What's your last name?"

"Lars," Neal said hoarsely.

"Birthday?" she asked.

Neal opened his mouth, and then he closed it. He couldn't remember his birthday.

"Oh Christ," he spat. "A god-damned head injury."

"It's alright," she said soothingly. "It's alright. Relax for me, alright?"

"BP just spiked, Cindy," Timmy said.

She nodded.

Another person arrived on the scene, and Neal heard a car door slam shut. Trooper Henry Martini jogged into view and came to squat down by him.

"Hey Neal," the younger man said. "Why don't you give me a description of the perp?"

Neal closed his eyes and realized he could picture Dylan perfectly. He couldn't remember his birthday, but he sure as hell could remember him.

And he told Henry all about the man.

CHAPTER 63

THE ACCIDENT, 9:15 AM, MAY 4TH, 2016

Brian looked into the parlor from the hallway and couldn't believe what he saw.

The front end of a pickup truck had smashed into the house. Debris was scattered everywhere, and the engine whined and spat. The horn blasted, and dust plaster hung heavy in the air. A figure was slumped over the steering wheel.

In a second, Brian and Jacob were climbing over broken furniture and shattered walls. Brian could hear Shane on the phone, calling in the accident. Jacob reached the truck's door and forced it open. Brian slipped past him, reached under the steering column, found the keys and turned off the engine. Blood dripped down from the driver's head, and the man looked beat to hell.

Jacob scrambled over to the other side of the pickup, pulled the passenger's side door open, and got in.

"Ready?" Jacob asked.

Brian nodded. Jacob gently moved the driver towards Brian, and Brian eased the man out of the truck. The stranger was slim and short. He also stank of vodka. The blood fell quickly from several wounds, and Brian hoped the man didn't have any blood-borne illnesses.

Suddenly, Shane was at his side, and the two of them got the driver out into the hall.

"The ambulance is on its way," Shane said as Jacob came out of the room with a blanket and a throw pillow. He slapped the dust off of them before he tossed them onto the floor. "Got a first-aid kit?"

Brian nodded. "Bathroom. Above the cabinet."

Shane helped Brian put the man on the pillow. As Shane left to get the first aid kit, Jacob looked at the driver.

"Doesn't look too bad," Jacob said. "Course, we can't really tell what's going on inside."

"Yeah," Brian agreed. "Hey, grab the blanket, will you?"

Jacob reached out, pulled it close and passed it over to Brian. Brian spread it out over the unconscious man. Shane was back a moment later, opening the kit while kneeling down.

Shane took out a steri-pad and tore the wrapper off.

And the man opened his eyes. He looked from Brian to Shane and then to Jacob, and the man smiled.

"Hey," Shane said softly. "You okay?"

"I'm fine," the man replied, slurring his words slightly. "Very good now, actually. How are the three of you doing?"

Brian took the question to be the product of shock or a traumatic brain injury, so he tried to keep the conversation light. "We're okay. Just worried about you. Can you tell me what your name is?"

"Oh yes," the man grinned, "I'm Josephus Wahlen."

CHAPTER 64

THE CALL, 9:17 AM, MAY 4TH, 2016

Henry Martini got up and walked away from Neal Lars. The part-time cop, full-time pain had taken an undeserved beating. Neal may have gotten a little too rough at times, but he never lied, it wasn't how the guy operated, and from what he had told Henry, Neal hadn't even deserved the beat down.

And, as much as he found Neal annoying, Lars was still a cop.

Henry rubbed at his chin. The description Neal had given sounded like Dylan Mailer, an amateur runner who liked to run drunk. The man had been stopped and cited a few times for drunk and disorderly, but never for an assault.

Henry's radio squawked as he approached the patrol car and he keyed the microphone. "Say again, dispatch?"

"We've got a report of a vehicle collision with a house," dispatch replied.

"Where?" Henry asked, getting into his cruiser.

"One Eighty-Five Old Nashua Road," dispatch answered. "It was a white pickup truck."

Henry paused his hands on the keys in the ignition. "Say again?"

"White pickup. No tags given," dispatch said.

"That's Lars' truck," Henry said. "The driver's got to be Dylan Mailer, I'm pretty sure he's the one who beat Neal down."

"Alright," dispatch said. "Putting the all-call out now. Be safe and approach with caution."

"Copy, dispatch, out."

Henry started the engine, dropped the car into gear and tore off for Old Nashua Road.

No one beats up a cop.

No one.

CHAPTER 65

AN UNWELCOME GUEST, 9:20 AM, MAY 4TH, 2016

Josephus Wahlen sat up and smiled cheerfully at the three men, all of whom had backed away from him. They were confused, unsure of themselves and of what to do.

Perfect, Josephus thought. Dylan screamed from his little corner. Josephus' borrowed body was beyond battered. It had sustained multiple broken bones, and he was certain it would collapse completely if his own will was not so powerful.

"How?" a bald man asked.

"How?" Josephus replied, laughing. "Revenge is a wonderful motivator. A force which has driven me forward for well over a century and a half."

He pushed himself to his feet and looked at the men. Josephus saw their confusion, their hesitation. He watched them exchange glances. None of them wished to harm Dylan's body. It was plain on their faces, and Josephus knew he had them.

CHAPTER 66

A PROBLEM, 9:23 AM, MAY 4TH, 2016

Brian swallowed dryly and looked at the man in front them.

No, Brian corrected himself. *Josephus is in there.*

The body Josephus had hijacked was battered and bloodied, and part of the scalp hung down to the right. A section of the skull was revealed, and Brian was surprised Josephus was upright.

Then again, Brian was surprised Josephus was there.

When Brian looked at Shane and Jacob, he saw his own worry reflected in their faces.

How do we stop him without hurting the person he possessed?

Before he could voice the question, Josephus attacked.

It was quick, and it was brutal.

Josephus moved faster than Brian expected, and Josephus grabbed hold of Jacob's throat. He lifted the man up, squeezing as he did so.

And Brian suddenly realized how strong Josephus was.

Shane leaped at Josephus, who swung Jacob and struck Shane with him. Brian jumped over Shane as the man slammed into the wall and collapsed. Josephus, grinning, lashed out with a leg and caught Brian in the stomach. Brian vomited his breakfast and choked as he staggered back, tripping over Shane and falling to the floor. As Shane struggled to get up, and Brian desperately tried to breathe, Josephus brought Jacob's face close to his own.

Jacob was kicking and punching viciously, but regardless of how many blows he landed, Josephus was unmoved. He kept a firm grip on Jacob's neck, not tight enough to kill the man, merely to hold him in place.

Jacob snarled at Josephus.

Josephus smiled, leaned forward, and bit off Jacob's nose. Blood exploded out of the wound, pouring down Jacob's face and spraying out across Josephus'. Josephus spat the nose out, and then he smashed Jacob's head onto the floor. He managed to do it twice before Shane was on top of him.

Brian, finally able to breathe, staggered forward.

Shane, straddling Josephus' back, was punching the man repeatedly in the back of the head. Brian kicked at Josephus' arms, yet nothing worked.

It was then that Brian realized the man's intention.

Josephus was strangling Jacob.

Brian lashed out with his foot, connecting solidly with Josephus' bicep, but the man continued to hold on.

Suddenly, Josephus stood up, knocking Shane back. But Shane scrambled up and threw a wild punch.

Josephus, grinning, caught Shane's fist. With a happy expression, Josephus squeezed and twisted.

The blood drained from Shane's face as his shoulder popped audibly, and sharp cracks rang out from Josephus' hand. Josephus chuckled and let go. Shane collapsed to the floor, unable to move, shock and horror on his face.

Josephus shook his head.

"I'm not seeing someone here, Brian," Josephus said, looking around.

"You didn't come for me?" Brian asked, wondering where Jenny was.

"Oh, I did," Josephus replied, licking Jacob's blood off his lips. "But more importantly, I have come to speak with your delectable wife. I must confess myself irritated with her behavior. I do not appreciate being shot. It was a most unpleasant experience. You will agree, I'm certain, that she must reap what she has sown."

"No," Brian said, "no, I don't agree at all."

His heart did a mad little dance in his chest, and stars exploded around the edges of his vision. He spat the last remnants of bile out of his mouth and prayed he wouldn't die of a heart attack before Jenny got away.

"Now, now," Josephus said soothingly, tucking the flap of scalp up behind his ear and smiling. "You are a good husband, so I can see, but she must be punished. Much like a child, a wife must be disciplined, kept in line. It is her duty, as told so righteously in the Good Book. And it is your duty, I might add, to ensure she is properly educated."

A siren interrupted Brian's response, and he looked out to the door. It was then that Josephus attacked.

CHAPTER 67

JENNY INTERVENES, 9:33 AM, MAY 4TH, 2016

Jenny had gotten to the desk and opened the top left drawer. She had taken out the snail-mail envelopes, thrown them down and retrieved Brian's Glock nine-millimeter semi-automatic. She had checked the magazine to make sure it was loaded, put a round into the chamber, and went and stood by the door.

She hadn't known it would be Josephus. She had suspected, but she also didn't want to run out with a loaded weapon if the driver had had a freak accident. Jenny had remained in the room as she heard Shane make the call for an ambulance. She had heard the men speak to the driver. And she had heard the man say who he was.

The fight had started only a few seconds later, and when she had quickly looked out of the study, she had seen the situation was too chaotic for her to shoot clearly. Instead of throwing herself into the mix, Jenny had stepped back into the study. She waited.

Her moment would come and she would shoot.

She would kill Josephus, and it didn't matter to her whether she killed the man he possessed or not.

Josephus was going to hurt her. He would try to use Brian to do it as well, but she wouldn't let him.

Every noise pained her, but she knew she needed to be patient.

And so she was. Jenny waited until she heard Josephus speak. It wasn't the voice she had heard on the phone. The possessed man's voice was thinner and higher. The tone, though, and the disdain which came through with each word, that was unmistakably Josephus.

He spoke to Brian about the need to correct her behavior. He said how she needed to be disciplined. The conversation continued briefly, but then it was cut short by the sound of a siren. And then she heard someone crash into the wall, and Josephus laughed.

Jenny stepped into the doorway of the study and brought the semi-automatic pistol up. Both hands were on the grip, the index finger of her right hand curled firmly around the trigger. She lined the sight up with Josephus' chest and waited for the man to notice her.

It only took a moment.

He stood in the center of the hallway. Jacob looked bloody and dead on the floor. Shane was near him, writhing in agony.

Brian was unconscious, Josephus holding him up by the collar.

"Jennifer!" Josephus said happily. "I'm so pleased you're here."

CHAPTER 68

THE CAVALRY ARRIVES, 9:33 AM, MAY 4TH, 2016

Henry Martini blocked the end of the driveway at one eighty-five Old Nashua Road and jumped out of his cruiser. He saw Neal Lars' truck, the back end of which was in the front yard while the nose and cab were firmly embedded in the old farmhouse.

Someone screamed, and Henry drew his weapon as he ran to the front steps. He raced up them and kicked open the door as he yelled, "State Police!"

The deadbolt ripped through the doorjamb and part of Henry recoiled in horror at what he saw. Two men were down, while a third dangled unconscious from the arm of a fourth. To the left was a woman, who had a Glock pointed at the fourth man.

And it was the fourth man who interested Henry the most; the man perfectly fit the description that Neal Lars had given.

Henry leveled his own pistol on Dylan, the assailant and said, "Sir, put the man down."

Dylan didn't even look at him. He was focused solely on the woman.

"Go away," Dylan said. "None of this concerns you. Jennifer and I have some issues to discuss."

Henry kept his eyes on Dylan, but he addressed the woman.

"Jennifer?" he said.

"Yes?" she asked. Her voice was calm, the gun steady in her hands.

"I'm going to ask you to lower your firearm and leave the building from another exit," Henry said.

"Oh no," Dylan said. "She can't leave. I have her husband. Her beloved Brian. If she leaves, I'll gut him like a fish and leave him screaming on the floor."

"No," Henry said. "You will not. You're going to carefully lower Brian to the floor. Am I understood?"

Dylan dropped his free hand to Brian's stomach and chuckled. "Have you ever seen a man's intestines pulled out before?"

Henry didn't answer. The situation was spiraling out of control. He needed to keep everything calm until other units arrived.

"No," Dylan said. "I don't believe you have. Very few people have actually had the pleasure of seeing it, let alone participating in the same. I find it to be one of life's little gifts. There is something truly wondrous about seeing a person's innards strung about like so much garland."

"Dylan," Henry said.

"Silence," Dylan snapped. All of the playfulness had left his voice. "This harlot and I have unfinished business to which I must attend. My time here, I have no doubt, is abysmally short. You can either retreat to a position of safety, or you can watch me kill Brian first, and then Jennifer.

"And if you should ruin my revenge," Dylan said, turning to look at Henry, "I shall have to appease myself with your sorry flesh."

Dylan's pupils seemed to *flicker*.

For the first time since arriving at the house, Henry was afraid. His palms began to sweat and his grip on the pistol loosened. He wanted to run to his car, get the AR-15 rifle out of the trunk and come back with it.

Just to be sure, he told himself.

A small voice in his gut told him the rifle might not be nearly enough.

CHAPTER 69

A Decision is Made, 9:40 AM, May 4th, 2016

Jenny kept her pistol on target. Chills ran through her as she listened to Josephus speak about eviscerating Brian. It wasn't from fear, though, but rage.

The more Josephus spoke, the deeper, more profound her anger became.

The world slowed down.

She couldn't hear anything the State Trooper or Josephus said. She became hypersensitive, and it looked as though the world was a film being advanced one frame at a time.

Josephus' hand moved with all of the speed of a sloth to hover above Brian's stomach. She watched as Josephus turned his head, quarter inch by quarter inch, to face the trooper. She saw his lips part and form words. She saw the trooper's eyes move casually from Josephus to Brian, and back to Josephus.

Jenny read the fear in the man's face, and she understood it.

But it wasn't the trooper's loved one who was being threatened.

Her Brian was there.

Without rushing, Jenny lowered her pistol and took careful aim on Josephus right elbow. She breathed in slowly, made sure her hands were steady and pulled the trigger.

Her ears barely registered the sound of the gun, but she saw the bullet explode out of the barrel. She could see the vapor trail as it hurtled towards Josephus.

And her aim was true.

The bullet struck.

The body Josephus had taken control of was thin. The body of a long distance runner. When the round punched through the joint, it neatly severed the lower arm from the upper. Blood sprayed out, and the arm dropped, the fingers locked on Brian's collar. Brian fell to the floor in slow motion and flopped slightly as he landed.

The condescending sneer on Josephus' face was replaced by a comical expression of surprise. Jenny watched the ejector of the pistol throw the empty brass casing in a high arc away from the weapon. Josephus turned to look at his severed arm, and the world slammed back into full speed.

With a shriek, Josephus lunged towards her.

Jenny emptied the rest of the Glock's clip into his chest, and the State Trooper did the same.

CHAPTER 70

IN A BOX

Josephus awoke to darkness.

Dylan, whom he had possessed, was dead.

But Josephus wasn't back in the crypt.

In fact, he didn't know where he was.

He tried to move but found he couldn't. He couldn't see or hear anything. Josephus gathered all of his strength and pushed himself as far as he could go. He was in a room lit by strange, long lights, and all of the surfaces seemed to be made of metal. He saw bodies on metal tables, all of them in the process of being cut into.

Josephus turned around and saw the pale, mangled form of Dylan. The severed forearm had been placed on the man's thin chest, which had a score of bloodless wounds.

Why am I here? Josephus wondered.

And then he found the answer; his bone. The one he had made Dylan swallow. It was still in the man's stomach. He was bound to the dead man's flesh. He needed more of himself if he was to regain his strength.

But how? Josephus thought.

A steel door in the far wall opened, and a tall, thin man with plain, ordinary features walked in. He looked like every man and like none. He walked purposefully to the first body, checked some paperwork attached to it, and then he moved on to the next.

Josephus felt a wave of relief at the sight of the man. Josephus gathered his thoughts and threw himself at the man's mind.

Yet nothing happened. The man was impervious. Unassailable. The man waved at his ear as though he shooed a fly away.

And then he moved on to the third body.

Josephus pushed again, yet in spite of his effort, the man did nothing.

The man stopped beside Dylan's body, picked up the papers, nodded, and then moved the table. As the table moved, so too did Josephus.

With terrible dismay, Josephus realized he had bound himself to a corpse.

CHAPTER 71

A BONFIRE, 9:30 PM, MAY 20TH, 2016

For a price, anything could be purchased.

Brian had found a professional spelunker who didn't ask questions, and who accepted cash payments. For a modest fee, the man had gone into the crypt, found the passage to the stream, and recovered every last bit of Josephus' remains. Said remains were in a duffel bag at Brian's feet.

He sat in an Adirondack chair in the backyard, swatting away a particularly annoying mosquito. Jenny was beside him, her hand in his, and Shane sat a few feet away. In a new fire pit, several large logs burned brightly. Sparks occasionally shot up when a knot in the wood burst and embers drifted up once in a while.

The three of them were drinking red wine, which Brian's cardiologist said he could drink. In moderation.

Shane's arm and hand were in a cast, and they would be so for a while. Brian was waiting for a couple of partial dentures to come in. Josephus had knocked several of them out.

Jenny had been forced to get a prescription sleep aid. Her nightmares about Josephus were sufficiently violent enough to force Brian to sleep in the spare bedroom.

The one who had suffered the worst, aside from the man who had been possessed, was Jacob Wurbach. Josephus had killed him. Shane, who seemed to have friends everywhere, was able to get Jacob buried in a small lot down in Nashua. Far, far away from Wood's Cemetery.

Brian was worried about Josephus, and he had even asked Leo to inspect the crypt before he sent the spelunker in. But the malicious ghost hadn't been there.

Nothing had been there. Leo hadn't even been able to find the shadow world Josephus had created.

Brian didn't trust it. None of it.

"You okay, babe?" Jenny asked, squeezing his hand.

"Hm?" he asked, looking over at her.

"Are you okay?" she said.

"Yeah," Brian replied. "Just wondering where Josephus is."

"I hope he's in hell," Shane said. He drank the last of his wine and set the empty wine glass down on the ground. "I mean, I really, really hope he's suffering in hell right now."

Jenny nodded her agreement.

Brian did the same as he let go of Jenny's hand and stood up. He set his own glass on the arm of his chair and picked up the duffel bag. He carried it over to the fire, squatted down and reached into the bag. One by one, he withdrew Josephus' bones, and he tossed them onto the wood. The smell was harsh, bringing tears to his eyes. Yet he continued to burn Josephus' remains.

Dark, oily smoke rose up from the flames, and the bones cracked as they burned. It took him a long time.

When he finally stood up, Jenny said from behind him, "Burn the bag too, Brian. Burn it all."

Wordlessly, Brian lifted the bag and tossed it onto the logs. As the fire ate at the fabric, he brushed his hands off on his jeans, walked back to his chair and sat down. Once more, his hand found Jenny's, and he took another drink of wine.

In silence, Brian, Jenny and Shane watched the flames.

CHAPTER 72

ST. JOSEPH'S CEMETERY, MILFORD, NH

Rich Deering stumbled out of the parking lot for the Milford Steak House. Annie, the bartender, had taken his keys. She had also called Kristy, his wife.

And Rich really, *really* didn't want to listen to Kristy complain about him being drunk. It was a man's right to be drunk.

Hell, he thought, *a man's got to get drunk once in a while.*

He had used the argument before. With limited success. Rich and Kristy had a fundamental disagreement as to what once in a while actually was. She believed it meant once or twice a year. Rich was a firm defender of several times a week. It made for some loud discussions at the house. Not to mention, him appearing in the police section of the Milford newspaper a couple of times a month for drunk and disorderly.

Rich wasn't going to wait for her to arrive. She'd complain the whole way home, then scream and yell at him once they were in the apartment, and eventually the cops would show up.

Nope, Rich told himself. *Not today.*

He looked around and saw the gate to St. Joseph's Cemetery was open. The weather was warm, he realized. A hint of summer in the night air.

No one will bother you in a graveyard, a soft voice whispered to him.

Rich nodded his agreement. No one ever went into cemeteries, not after dark. Too afraid. It would be a great place to sleep one off. He could always make his way home in the morning after Kristy left for work. No, the cemetery was looking good.

Damn good.

Smiling happily to himself, Rich walked to the edge of the parking lot. He wasn't drunk enough to not look both ways. When he was certain the way was clear, he crossed the road and fell when he reached the break-down lane. For a minute, he lay in the sand of the shoulder, looking up at the night sky. The stars and the moon were bright, and Rich smiled.

"Beautiful," he murmured. He closed his eyes. He was tired.

No, the little voice in his head whispered, *you can't sleep here. She might find you.*

Rich's eyes snapped open. He definitely didn't want to be found on the side of the road by Kristy. He would never hear the end of it. She would probably start in on the whole rehab clinic again.

Like I'll ever go there, Rich snorted. He rolled onto his stomach and managed to get himself up on his feet after several attempts. He brushed the sand off of himself clumsily, and stumbled his way into the cemetery.

Now, he thought, looking around. *Where to sleep?*

Several mausoleums looked good. He could tuck himself in behind one and get some decent shut-eye and not have to worry about Kristy. She loved to wake him up when he had a hangover.

Rich headed for the closest building, but as he did so, the little voice spoke up again.

What if she comes in here? the voice asked. *She'll look at big places. The places up front. You should go to the back. No one ever looks out back.*

Rich couldn't argue with the voice's logic, and he wondered, for a minute, how he had gotten so smart.

Must have been the Schnapps, he thought, grinning.

Usually, he didn't drink it, but Matt had been buying. And when someone's buying, you drink whatever they put in front of you.

Rich wandered through the cemetery, which was bigger than he had suspected. The moonlight lit up the headstones and the grass, the paved roads. He made his way steadily to the back, and he saw newer markers. Bright, polished stones. In the far right corner of the cemetery, he saw the perfect spot.

A new headstone. Not too tall. But nice and wide. Perfect to hide behind.

Rich was able to read the name on the marker. Dylan Mailer.

"Hope you don't mind company, Dylan," Rich said, chuckling.

But as he sat down at the grave something strange happened; Rich lost control of himself.

His body twisted around so he was on all fours. He ripped up handfuls of grass until the turf came up in sheets. The smell of fresh earth filled his nose as his hands plunged into the dirt. He dug quickly, and steadily, and he was unable to stop himself. Rich tried to get his hands to listen, to make any part of himself listen, but as he did so, the little voice which had told him so many excellent ideas, spoke up.

And it wasn't little anymore.

I don't need you for long, the voice said. *Only for a short while, I promise. We have some digging to do.*

Why? Rich thought, panic welling up in him.

I need something, something in the coffin. But don't worry, the voice said, *it will be easy to find.*

What is it? Rich asked.

Just keep digging, the voice said soothingly.

Rich's hands continued their excavation. He had formed a rough rectangle and worked down, casting handfuls of dirt out onto the grass.

Is it in the grave? Rich asked, horrified.

Yes, the voice said.

Somewhere in the casket? Rich said.

Indeed, it is, the voice said, chuckling.

Will it be easy to get? Rich asked, desperately hoping he was having a nightmare.

It depends on how you might view the task, the voice said. *Have you fished before, Richard?*

Yes, Rich answered.

Has a fish ever swallowed a hook? the voice asked. *And have you had to retrieve it?*

Yes, Rich replied. *Did you lose a hook?*

No, the voice laughed. *Not at all. But what I need is in Dylan's stomach. Let us hope, for your sake, that they did not stitch him up too well. I would hate for you to have to chew your way in.*

Rich screamed within his own head as his hands continued to dig.

Yet even as the stranger forced Rich's body to dig faster, Rich felt something happening within his head. A pulsing and throbbing in his right temple. He didn't know what it was, but he could tell it was bad. The farther he dug, the worse it became. Beneath the stranger's control, Rich could feel his heartbeat changing, thundering erratically. It felt as though his heart was a fist and it sought to batter its way out of his chest. The vein in his right temple continued its own mad rhythm, and then one in his left temple joined in.

He felt his fingernails crack, and the pinky finger on his right hand broke. Rich's lungs screamed for oxygen and his stomach rebelled at the labor. He threw up. The vomit, a foul mixture of alcohol and bar snacks. It turned the dirt into a muddy mixture as mucus ran from his nostrils and tears streamed from his eyes.

Rich's arms shook and he knew it wasn't from the digging.

I'm going to die, Rich realized dimly.

Not yet, the voice said conversationally. *I'm not done with you.*

Before Rich could reply someone spoke.

"It's true, Leo" a woman said, and Rich looked up.

A middle-aged, attractive woman stood on the right side of the grave. Beside her was a smaller man, and while she had a sympathetic expression, the man's was one of polite curiosity.

"Josephus is in the man," the woman said.

Leo nodded. "Yes, Sylvia, you are absolutely correct."

From a darkened section of the cemetery road, a man appeared, stocky and bald. He carried with him a plastic shopping bag and a shovel. The stranger within Rich's head began screaming in rage.

Suddenly, Leo and Sylvia reached down and took hold of Rich, their hands painfully cold on his wrists. The stranger shrieked, blasphemies and curses spewing, ricocheting through Rich's mind. Despite the freezing grip they had upon him, Leo and Sylvia were gentle, even as the stranger tried to force Rich's arms to shake them off. When they had taken him out of the hole he had dug, the bald man reached them, nodded to Sylvia and Leo, and dropped the bag to the ground.

Rich didn't see any more, for the one named Leo leaned over him and reached into his chest. The sensation was shocking, a bitter chill that fished through his flesh. Rich could feel the hands digging inside him. The questing fingers searched for the stranger and finally grabbed hold of him and tugged forcefully.

Horrified, and quickly becoming sober, Rich watched as a dull white form was dragged from his chest. In a moment, it formed into the bare semblance of a man, and the stranger attempted to fight Leo. Yet even as the stranger attacked the other man, Sylvia stepped in. The three forms melded and shifted, the earth shuddering beneath them. Grass turned white and broke, tree limbs shook and frozen leaves plummeted to the ground.

The sound of a shovel, striking something hard, caught Rich's attention and he twisted around, wincing at the pain in his arms and hands.

At the grave, he saw the bald man, who threw the shovel out of the grave. He reached out, found where he had dropped the bag and dragged it into the hole. Within a minute, the man in the grave climbed out, with the bag and nodded pleasantly to Rich.

Rich could only nod back.

The man squatted down, opened the bag and pulled out a small object, which Rich couldn't quite make out.

"Sylvia," the bald man said, "I've got it. It was just one bone, right?"

From behind Rich, the woman Sylvia said, "Yes, Shane."

"Fair enough," Shane said. He placed the bone on the ground, removed a container of salt from the bag and shook some of it out onto both earth and the bone. Next, he took a bottle of lighter fluid out and sprayed the bone and the ground around with the liquid. A moment later, he pulled a box of matches from the bag, and a scream forced Rich to twist around.

The stranger who had been drawn from Rich's chest was shrieking. Leo and Sylvia were on either side of the pale form, each holding an arm. The figure had lost much of its substance, and Rich could see a great deal of the cemetery through him.

"You cannot!" the stranger howled. "You must not!"

The striking of a match was the only response.

A moment later, the sound of flames devouring oxygen, filled the night air.

The thing which had hijacked Rich's body shrieked. A terrible, agonized sound which threatened to shatter Rich's eardrums. The figure writhed and twisted, seeking to escape. But neither Leo nor Sylvia let go.

He rolled away from the shrieking shape and looked back at the bald man. The man lit a cigarette as the flames reflected brightly in his pale skin. He saw Rich looking at him, and he smiled.

Around his cigarette, Shane chuckled and said, "Only way to get rid of him."

Rich dry-heaved once, and fainted, the sounds of fire and screams chasing him into unconsciousness.

CHAPTER 73
BRIAN AND JENNY AND THE CEMETERY

Brian and Jenny sat on the hood of her car, staring into Wood's Cemetery. They were parked just outside of the gate and each of them was armed with a shotgun. Each shell was loaded with rock salt, and Brian felt a nervous flutter in his stomach.

What if the bone in Dylan's body isn't the last? he wondered. *What if there are more?*

"Are you okay?" Jenny asked, glancing over at him.

Brian nodded, "Worried is all."

"Me too," she said. She slid a little closer to him, adjusting her grip on the weapon. "How will we know if it worked?"

Before Brian could answer, the earth rumbled. A slight tremor which shook the car and caused the chain around the gates to rattle. Then, at the far edge of his vision, where the moonlight shined brightly down upon the Paupers' Crypt, Brian saw movement. Dim, gray shapes drifted up from the grass. After a moment, he saw the shapes were people. Vague outlines of those who had been buried and trapped by Josephus.

They were moving up, through the air, and towards the heavens.

"It worked," Brian said softly, pulling Jenny in close. "Thank God, Jenny, it worked."

* * *

Woods Cemetery, August 1st, 1971

Jacob Wurbach walked to the office door, opened it and went into the building.

The heat within was heavy and humid, exactly the same as it was in the cemetery itself.

And Jacob loved it.

His blood had thinned after two years in Vietnam. He had also come home with a vicious case of malaria, as well as a form of 'jungle rot' the dermatologists in Boston were still fascinated by.

He set Gary Winn's order and wondered where the man was.

It was unlike Gary to be gone when Jacob brought in the goods. Jacob was the only other man from Mont Vernon who had seen combat overseas. Gary had fought the Vietcong up on the Cambodian border, and Jacob had fought them on the coast.

Terrible times Jacob would like to forget, but his nightmares kept images of the war at the forefront of his thoughts most days.

Jacob glanced out the window over the desk, saw Gary's beat-up old Chevy parked on the grass, and wondered where the man was. The doors to the bathroom and the closet were both open.

Jacob paused.

The double barrel shotgun, Gary kept around for the raccoons, wasn't in the closet. On the floor by the desk was a package; the brown paper ripped free to reveal boxes and boxes of shells for the gun.

Jacob reached down, took a box out and looked at it.

Each shell was loaded with rock salt.

Jacob put the box back and walked to the doorway. He looked out at the cemetery and tried to spot Gary.

Where in the hell did he get off to? Jacob wondered.

Two quick blasts answered the question.

A moment later, Gary came running from the back right corner.

Gary stopped, broke the weapon down, reloaded it with shells from his shirt pocket, turned and took aim.

Jacob tried to see what Gary had run from, and stiffened.

Harold Morgen was walking up from the old Paupers' Crypt.

The problem was Harold had been killed when a tree fell on him back in nineteen thirty-three, and since the Morgen family was poorer than dirt, Harold had been buried in the Paupers' Crypt.

The man's skin was sickeningly white, his eyes blacker than night in the jungle.

He was grinning. His long white teeth, which had always scared Jacob as a boy, flashed in the morning light.

Gary fired both barrels and Harold vanished.

When Gary turned and saw Jacob, he yelled, "Get out, Jacob! Get the hell out of here!"

Jacob didn't wait around to ask why.

He leaped out of the doorway and raced towards the exit, only to see the gates slam shut on their own.

Jacob skidded to a stop, caught a glimpse of movement out of his right eye and turned in time to see a corpse pull herself out of an old slate headstone.

The lady looked even worse than Harold had.

Her skin was dark gray, the nails as black as her eyes. The lips around her open mouth were a putrid white, and she stank of death. A smell the war had made Jacob all too familiar with.

She was a short, thin woman, and whether her slim figure was from being buried for so long or the way she was in life, Jacob couldn't tell.

He didn't care either.

Her gap-toothed smile was far from friendly.

The shotgun ripped the air, and the woman vanished even as Jacob let out a howl of pain.

"Jacob!" Gary yelled. "Back to the office!"

Again Jacob didn't argue, he turned and sprinted towards the office.

There were dead everywhere. Gary was at the office door, weapon ready. He stepped aside as Jacob hurtled in, tripped, rolled and slammed into the far wall while Gary kicked the door closed and locked it.

"Oh thank Christ," Gary said. "Catch."

Jacob sat up and caught the shotgun.

"It's loaded," Gary said without looking back at Jacob.

Jacob put his back against the wall, kept the barrels of the weapon pointed at the closed door and asked, "What in God's name is going on out there, Gary?"

"Hold on," Gary said, ripping into the box of goods Jacob had delivered. "Ah, perfect."

He pulled out a large box of Morton's salt, cracked it open and laughed. He slammed the window closed and poured a thick line of salt across the sash and the sill.

Jacob watched as he did the same thing at the threshold. He then went around the small office and filled the corners and lined the walls with it as well. Finally, Gary walked back to the desk, dropped the empty Morton's container to the floor and pulled out a pair of beers. He gave one to Jacob and then he sat down.

"Thanks," Jacob said, handing the shotgun back to Gary. He popped the top on the beer, took a big swallow and said, "What the hell is going on?"

"Something terrible," Gary said, opening his own beer. "Something absolutely terrible, Jacob. It'll be worse if the damned fog rolls in."

"Fog?" Jacob asked. "In August?"

Gary looked over the can at him, lowered it and said. "It's not a natural fog."

"What do you mean?" Jacob said. "What the hell are you talking about?"

"Remember when we were ten, and the Conrad boy went missing?" Gary asked.

"Timmy Conrad?" Jacob said. "I remember. He showed up a year later. Some crazy story about being trapped in the cemetery the whole time. Didn't his sister say they think he ran off with the circus that came through Manchester, the summer before?"

"Timmy wasn't lying," Gary said.

"What?" Jacob asked. "Are you trying to tell me Timmy Conrad was hiding here for a year and no one noticed?"

"He wasn't hiding," Gary said. "Timmy came along last September when I was discharged and got this job. Wanted to talk to me about the cemetery."

"Oh yeah?" Jacob said. "Where's he at now?"

"He converted to Catholicism and became a priest. Served as a chaplain with the Navy during the first year of Vietnam," Gary answered. "Not the point, though. See, he wanted to tell me about what could happen here. Said this was a bad place. A place where evil was strong. He told me he was trapped here for a year until the fog drifted away and he was able to get out."

"Gary," Jacob said, "what the hell does this have to do with what just happened?"

"I'm getting there, I'm getting there," Gary said. "This place, Timmy said, keeps the dead trapped here. They can't get away. It was their spirits we saw. And they're angry. Every once in a while, a fog rolls in from the marsh wraps itself around the cemetery, and keeps people, living people, trapped inside."

"Timmy Conrad told you this?" Jacob asked.

Gary nodded.

"Listen," Jacob said. "I'm not doubting we saw something strange out there. Hell, I know Harold Morgen's dead. I remember seeing him when they brought him in after the accident. And I figure none of those other folks were too lively either. Fog, though? And being trapped here for a year?"

"Yes," Gary said. "Listen, I thought Timmy was a little off when he came here and told me the story. It was the look in his eyes, though, Jacob. He was telling the truth. And nothing but the truth."

Jacob took a long drink of beer, held onto the can and stood up to look out the window.

"Oh Jesus," Jacob said softly.

"What?" Gary asked.

"Look."

TIMMY CONRAD TOLD THE TRUTH

Gary got up and stood beside Jacob.

"God in Heaven," Gary whispered.

Jacob nodded.

Beyond the window, and a half a dozen feet away from the office, stood more dead than he could count. Some were deathly white, others dark gray, many more were varying shades of the same. But all had black eyes.

It hadn't been the dead which had made Jacob upset.

The dead he had accepted. As nightmarish as the ghosts were, Jacob had no choice but to accept them. One had come after him, and he had seen Gary rid the day of it.

For some reason, though, Jacob hadn't wanted to admit the possibility of a fog which acted against nature.

Fog on an August day? One which rolled on in and trapped people in a cemetery? he wondered.

Now, Jacob didn't have a choice but to believe.

Beyond the dead, beyond the iron fence, a sturdy wall of fog reached from the summer grass to a dark sky. The temperature had dropped sharply. The world, as Jacob knew it, had been shrunk to the size of the cemetery.

"Holy Christ, Jacob, you're bleeding," Gary said, surprised.

Jacob looked down at his right arm and saw blood on his sleeve. For the first time, he felt the warm fluid against his skin, and pain in his flesh. He smelled the thick, coppery scent of blood.

"Did I hit you with the rock salt?" Gary asked.

"Must have," Jacob said. "Stings something fierce."

"Not surprised," Gary said. "Sit back down. I've got some iodine and plaster in the bathroom."

Jacob finished his beer, turned his attention away from the ghosts and fog, and sat down on the floor again. Gary went into the small bathroom, grabbed what he needed out of the medicine cabinet and brought them out. He hunkered down beside Jacob.

"Get your shirt off," Gary said.

He did so and tossed it over to the desk. He twisted his right arm slightly so Gary could get a better look at it. Eleven small holes bled steadily, each wound pulsing in time to his heart.

Gary shook his head. "Sorry, 'bout that."

"Not the first time I've been shot," Jacob said.

Gary chuckled, opened up the iodine and painted the injuries with it. Jacob wrinkled his nose at the smell, ignored the sting, and waited for Gary to slap the plaster on the holes. When Gary finished and put everything away, he said, "Should hold you for a bit."

"Thanks," Jacob said. "Don't know if it'll matter much, with the fog out there."

Gary nodded and sat back down. He cradled the shotgun and glanced at the door.

"What was with all the salt?" Jacob asked.

"Hm? Oh, yeah, the salt," Gary said, glancing around the room. "Well, it was one of the things Timmy told me. He said salt and iron keeps the dead at bay."

"And so the rock salt in the shells?" Jacob said.

"Exactly," Gary said. "See, I'd been noticing some strange things. Out of the corner of my eye, I thought I saw faces peering out of the headstones. Made me think maybe Timmy wasn't just right about the fog, but about the dead, too. Put an order in with McGuire's down in Nashua, came in yesterday with the post."

Jacob fished his Lucky Strikes and Zippo out of his pants pocket, shook out a cigarette and lit it up. He handed the pack and lighter to Gary, who took them with a nod of thanks.

"So you just decided to wander around the cemetery with a shotgun loaded with rock salt today?" Jacob asked after Gary handed the cigarettes and Zippo back.

"No," Gary said, exhaling a long cloud of smoke. "Heard something strange over at the Paupers' Crypt. Didn't even think too much of ghosts. Thought maybe it was an animal. Worse, maybe the Thomason boys. They've been raising hell this summer. Caught 'em twice trying to get in over the back fence."

"They're miserable kids," Jacob agreed.

"Anyway," Gary said, "I went down back this morning figuring to scare them off. Found the door to the crypt open. I looked in, and saw my first ghost. Scared the absolute hell out of me."

"Who was it?" Jacob asked, morbidly curious.

Gary shook his head. "Didn't know him. Older fella, dressed in an old black suit. Well, I asked him if he was alright, and when he stepped into the light I realized he wasn't. I fired both barrels without thinking."

"And he disappeared?" Jacob asked.

"Yup," Gary said. "I went to close the door over, but then Harold Morgen appeared. I took off running, stopped, reloaded, and let off a single shot. Didn't want to be caught off-guard again."

"I appreciate you doing that," Jacob said. "I expect something unpleasant happens otherwise?"

Gary looked at him for a moment, then he said, "Yeah. Timmy talked about it as well."

"Well," Jacob said, "what did Timmy say would happen?"

"I guess another fella got trapped in the cemetery, maybe six months after Timmy," Gary said. "Drifter looking for a place to sleep. Evidently, the cemetery didn't appreciate it. Before Timmy was able to get the guy to his hiding place, one of the ghosts managed to grab the man. He broke free and hid out with Timmy for a couple of days. But where the ghost had grabbed him, well, it was a bluish white. And it spread. After the first day, it had taken over most of his body. By the end of the second, the man died."

"What was it?" Jacob asked.

"Timmy said he didn't learn until he was in the war. Saw a couple of sailors who were rescued after being at sea in an open boat for a while. They had frostbite," Gary said. "Timmy said it was the same thing he'd seen on the drifter."

"Frostbite doesn't spread," Jacob said.

"Dead aren't supposed to rise either," Gary said evenly.

Jacob nodded. "Fair point there, Gary. Fair point."

Silence fell over them and then Jacob said, "They still out there?"

Gary got up and sat back down. "Yup."

"So, what do we do, just wait it out in the office?" Jacob asked.

"I suspect," Gary replied. "Can't see anything else to do. Except maybe tomorrow, if your arm's not too tight, we can try and make a break for it."

"Over the fence?" Jacob asked.

"Yeah," Gary said. "Think we can get over it, try to make it through the fog. Better than sitting in here and starving to death."

"Speaking of starving to death," Jacob said. "How the hell did Timmy survive a year?"

Gary looked at him and said, "Jacob, you don't want to know."

NIGHT COMES

For hours, Jacob and Gary swapped stories about the war. Each man fights his own war and has his own memories. Some of them he can share with men he served with, or who fought in the same theater.

Jacob's war, he remembered, was hate and rage and fear, all rolled into one great big mess. Day after day of slogging it through jungles and villages. Not able to sleep because you knew the Vietcong were going to come.

You knew they'd knife you, leave you alive and cut you up a little more as the moon went down, Jacob thought.

The Vietcong did terrible things to their prisoners, and Jacob had sworn never to be taken alive.

Jacob's war had been one without mercy, and it had left its mark.

Just like Gary going over the border in Cambodia and Laos had left its mark.

Those things they couldn't talk about with other people. They didn't understand.

And now they had something else people wouldn't understand.

Being trapped in the cemetery.

Jacob glanced at the office's sole window and wondered about the curious twilight beyond the glass.

He knew it was after nightfall. His watch confirmed it. Ten thirty. But there was no darkness, no moon, and no stars.

Nothing, Jacob realized, was as it should be.

Gary dozed in a corner, the shotgun on his lap. The man slept silently, perfectly still, as if he were dead.

Jacob's stomach rumbled, and he took a small drink of water from the beer can. The liquid was warm and pleasant, although it had a strong aftertaste of beer in it.

He put the can back on the floor and turned to the window again, only to have his heart leap within his chest.

A face looked in the window.

A child's face, dark gray, the eyes were a deep, horrific black Jacob had seen far too many times that day.

The child, a boy it seemed, had long white hair and a terrible grin. Several teeth were missing, but the remaining ones were hideously bright. A small hand appeared in the window beside the boy and waved.

Jacob raised his own hand and waved in return.

The grin turned into a genuine smile of delight. The child's sweet, young voice penetrated the glass.

"You're nice," the boy said. "I will kill you fast."

And then he disappeared.

Jacob processed the words, shook his head and took another drink.

"Did you say something?" Gary asked.

Jacob looked over at him. "No. We had a peeping tom."

"Oh yeah?" Gary said, sitting up and stretching. "Who?"

"Don't know," Jacob answered. "Dead kid. Said I was nice. So he'd kill me quick."

"Hell," Gary said, chuckling. "What a thoughtful thing to do."

"Yeah," Jacob said, grinning. He almost laughed, but he knew it would be full of panic and fear.

"Did you sleep at all?" Gary asked.

"No," Jacob said. He lit a cigarette, saw he had one more and passed it over to Gary. They lit up and smoked in silence for a few minutes.

"This is bad," Gary said.

Jacob nodded his agreement.

"There are a lot of ways a soldier can die," Gary said softly, his eyes locking onto the far wall. "Being murdered by a bunch of ghosts, well, it's certainly new."

"True," Jacob said. "I'd hate like hell to give them any sort of satisfaction, though."

"Me too," Gary said, grinning. He finished his cigarette, looked at the butt wistfully for a moment, and then crushed it against the floor board.

"Try to get some sleep, Jacob. We'll need all of our strength in the morning."

Gary cradled the shotgun, closed his eyes, and went back to sleep.

Jacob finished his own cigarette and looked to the window again.

Once more the boy was there, smiling at him.

Jacob shook his head, smiled, and waved.

Again the boy waved, and he began to sing.

It was an old hymn, and the child's voice was beautiful.

Jacob stretched out on the floor, smiling. He closed his eyes, interlocked his fingers on his chest and let the dead boy sing him to sleep.

MAKING A RUN FOR IT

Even though Jacob's watch said it was half past six in the morning, the twilight still remained.

As did the dead.

While several ghosts were close to the office, notably the dead boy and a pair of dead girls who looked like twins, the majority were near the fence. It was as though they knew what Jacob and Gary intended to do.

Regardless, the two men were going to try and escape anyway.

They ate the last of the food and drank the remainder of the beer. Both of them stuffed their pockets with shells for the shotgun. The plan was simple, with plenty of room for any necessary adaptation during its execution.

Open the door, blast the two nearest ghosts and run like hell.

Gary would fire first, break the gun open, and hand the weapon to Jacob, who would have a pair of shells ready. Jacob would remove the spent shells, load the fresh ones, fire, and return the shotgun to Gary, who would repeat the process.

They would aim for the closest section of fence. Whoever had the gun would put down a covering fire. The one who didn't would go over the iron and drop down. The shotgun would be passed through the fence and the unlucky one still in the cemetery would climb out while the other covered him.

Simple.

Not foolproof, of course, both men were too combat savvy to know nothing was ever foolproof.

They just hoped it wouldn't cost them their lives.

Silently, they walked to the door. Jacob grabbed hold of the handle and looked at Gary.

Gary shifted his grip on the shotgun, swallowed once and nodded.

With a quick twist and a shove, Jacob threw the door wide and pressed himself against the door frame. He had two shells in his hand and was ready when Gary fired two quick shots, broke the weapon open and tossed it to him.

Jacob caught it easily, ignored the heat of the barrel and the spent shells as Gary sprinted past him.

In a heartbeat, Jacob had the weapon loaded, ready and aimed, taking out a young man and a middle-aged matron who had been closing in on Gary. When Gary heard the second blast, he dug out a pair of shells and was ready when Jacob tossed it to him.

But the dead were not standing idly by.

They were racing towards the men.

Dozens had taken up positions along the fence and called out cheerfully to the men. The little boy who had peeked through the window was among them, and he jumped up and down excitedly.

"This isn't going to work," Jacob said as Gary fired off two quick shots and threw the weapon back, the two of them coming to a stop.

"No," Gary agreed, looking around quickly. "The crypt. Follow me."

He sprinted away, and Jacob got off two more shots before he ran after him.

Jacob's breath came in great gasps. He was no longer conditioned, he left all of it behind when he left the service.

And he was paying for it.

He followed close on Gary's heels, avoiding the grasping hands of the dead.

Laughter chased along after them, the dead gleeful in their pursuit.

Gary rounded the hill and let out a horrific scream as he ran into the embrace of a large, fat dead man. The man wrapped his large arms around Gary, who shrieked and writhed in agony.

Jacob reloaded and fired.

Part of the shot ripped off Gary's right ear, but the dead man vanished, and Gary fell to his knees. Jacob quickly replaced the shells, and got ready to fire again.

But the dead had backed off.

Their mocking laughter filled the suddenly cool air of the cemetery, the sound echoing off the fog.

Jacob dropped to a knee and put his hand on Gary's back as the man vomited into the grass. Gary was cold to the touch, even through his work shirt.

"Gary?" Jacob said.

Gary collapsed onto the ground, rolling away from his own vomit.

"Oh, Jesus, Gary," Jacob said softly.

Gary's neck was a bluish gray, as was his left cheek and part of his forehead. The left eye was black. Gary shivered and looked at Jacob. "I am freezing right now."

Jacob could only nod. He watched as the strange color spread slowly. A quarter of an inch at a time. Gary lay on his back, staring up at the clouds. His breath became labored. His lips turned a light blue.

Jacob knew Gary was dying. He had seen plenty of men do it before.

Within a short time Gary began to wheeze. A rattle filled each breath, his chest rising and falling weakly.

Gary clutched at the grass, his body going into spasms.

Jacob could only sit by him.

The dead had remained away, and Jacob couldn't imagine why.

Then, from around the small hill, the little boy with the white hair appeared.

For the first time, Jacob noticed the boy wore an elegant three-piece black suit. There was darker embroidery on the waistcoat and the lapels of the coat. The boy's shoes were highly polished and black with small buttons on the outside of each.

Jacob did not point the shotgun at him.

"Hello," he said, giving the boy a small wave. It was curious, for even though the boy was dead, and he knew the boy wished to kill him, Jacob felt no malice towards him.

"Hello," the boy replied. He came to a stop twenty feet away. "I haven't asked you your name."

"I'm Jacob," he said. "I'd shake your hand, but I don't want to die."

"We all die, Jacob," the boy said seriously. "But my name is Randy."

"A pleasure, Randy," Jacob said. He looked down at Gary, who lay with his eyes closed. His chest barely moved. The rattling, wheezing cough which heralded death filled the air.

"It won't be much longer now," Randy said.

"I know," Jacob replied. "He was a good man."

"We were curious about what you would do," Randy said after a moment.

Jacob frowned. "What do you mean?"

"Whether you would leave your friend, or stay with him," Randy answered. "There have been others who, when presented with this situation, have left their fallen friends."

"I wouldn't do it," Jacob said.

"Evidently," Randy said, grinning. "Remember my promise?"

"You'll kill me quickly?" Jacob asked.

Randy nodded happily. "It will be soon."

Jacob glanced down at Gary. "I know."

Randy turned and walked away.

Within a few minutes, Gary shuddered, struggled for a last breath, and then he went still.

The man was dead.

Silently Jacob went through Gary's pockets and took out the last half a dozen shotgun shells, stuffing them into his own pockets.

Jacob got up to his feet, his legs aching from the running. He looked around and saw the dead.

They stood in a wide arc with little space between them. It was as if they sought to keep him enclosed by the crypt.

Too many of them, Jacob realized, *I'll have no chance to shoot my way out.*

The grass rustled beside him.

Jacob turned in surprise and looked down.

A woman was pulling herself up and out of the ground beside Gary's corpse. She turned her head from left to right, stretched and stifled a yawn.

"Hello," she said, smiling.

Jacob stepped out of reach and looked in horror at her.

She climbed to her feet, her smile shifting into a grin. "I think it's your turn now."

"For what?" Jacob asked, leveling the shotgun at her gut.

"To die, of course," she said.

Jacob pulled both triggers and blasted her.

The woman vanished before his eyes and an enraged scream tore through the air.

Jacob threw the shotgun down as he turned and sprinted for the fence.

A howl of anger rose up from the throats of the dead and Jacob knew they pursued him.

He reached the wrought iron fence first, leaped and caught the cross piece. Old, jagged and rusted edges cut into his palms, but he ignored the pain as he pulled himself up. The wounds on his right arm opened, and fresh blood spilled down onto the iron. The fence's sharpened points scraped along his chest, digging in deep and drawing blood.

As he thrust himself over the top, he had a chance to see Woods Cemetery spread out before him.

The dead were nearly at the fence, and the pure rage and hatred in their faces made him nauseous with fear.

For a moment, he teetered on the top, bleeding and frightened.

Finally, he realized they could pull him back in, and Jacob swung his legs all the way over. He couldn't steady himself, or slow his fall, so he landed with a harsh thud onto the ground. Without hesitation, he rolled a few feet away, just out of the reach of the dead. They came to a stop at the fence and stood silently, impotently on the other side of the iron bars.

They seethed with rage, and Jacob knew they would tear him to pieces if he were any closer.

Yet not all of them were angry.

Randy stood near the front, a smile on his small face.

Jacob couldn't help himself as he smiled back.

With a great deal of difficulty, Jacob got to his feet. The fog was cold around him. A terrible feeling. His wounds continued to bleed, but he knew he couldn't stay where he was. He had to move.

He had to see if he could get home.

Jacob turned his back to the cemetery, to the dead and wandered out into the dense, white nothingness.

* * *

Check out these best-selling series from our talented authors:

GHOST STORIES

RON RIPLEY

BERKLEY STREET SERIES
MOVING IN SERIES
HAUNTED COLLECTION SERIES
DEATH HUNTER SERIES

IAN FORTEY

JIGSAW OF SOULS SERIES
CULT OF THE ENDLESS NIGHT SERIES

SUPERNATURAL SUSPENSE

A. I. NASSER

SLAUGHTER SERIES
SIN SERIES

DAVID LONGHORN

NIGHTMARE SERIES
ASYLUM SERIES

SARA CLANCY

THE BELL WITCH SERIES
BANSHEE SERIES

For a complete list of our new releases and best-selling horror books, visit
ScareStreet.com or scan the QR code below!

www.ingramcontent.com/pod-product-compliance
Lightning Source LLC
Chambersburg PA
CBHW050344030726
47503CB00008B/2611